A DOUBLE LIFE

Kay Barrenger was young, divorced...and broke! Among her material possessions in the suburb of Greenhill were her house, and her six-year-old son, Donnie. Her less material possessions included a good reputation...too good for the would-be matchmakers of Greenhill! All efforts were aimed at removing Kay from the ranks of the unattached.

Kay was amused by the efforts toward steering her into marriage, but she was bored with being a penurious alimony gaterer. She needed something to add spark to her life...and a little cash along the way wouldn't hurt a bit. That's when she began to write...

A DOUBLE LIFE

A Double Life

by
Daoma Winston

Magna Large Print Books
Long Preston, North Yorkshire,
England.

British Library Cataloguing in Publication Data.

Winston, Daoma
    A double life.

A catalogue record for this book is
available from the British Library

ISBN 0-7505-0482-X

First published in Great Britain by Severn House Publishers
Ltd., 1991

Copyright © 1970 by Daoma Winston

The right of Daoma Winston to be identified as the author
of this work has been asserted by her in accordance with
the Copyrights, Designs and Patents Act, 1988.

Published in Large Print 1993 by arrangement with Severn
House Publishers Ltd.

Printed and bound in Great Britain by
T.J. Press (Padstow) Ltd., Cornwall, PL28 8RW.

For Ray Winston

CONTENTS

1	Goodbye, Sam	11
2	Hello, Sex	44
3	Door To A Double Life	65
4	Enter The Worried Parents	82
5	The CSTB	110
6	Trapped	125
7	A Plot Presents Itself	141
8	A Crusader Comes	158
9	Blow-Out	174
10	The Teachers	191
11	Return Of The Crusader	202
12	Several Moments Of Truth	214
13	Certain Suspicions Confirmed	231
14	Dangerous Success	251
15	The Razor's Edge	265
16	Cupid Plots	279
17	Stormy Weather	295
18	Truths Win Out	310

CHAPTER 1

Goodbye, Sam

'Come on,' Sam said, and nudged Kay's shoulder. 'I'm sorry it took so long. We'll probably be late at the Devlins' now. Only what can you do? These people just don't have any system at all. What a business! Anyway, I've finally found it. We can go.'

She remained rooted before the paperback stand, her amber eyes slyly slanted at the display, at one particular cover in the display. That one particular cover was quite well-designed, she thought. A small blond girl on her knees. A tall, dark-haired man bending over her. His shirt was open to his waist, revealing solid muscle faintly shadowed. Very virile that.

She considered further, masked her delight, and stood unmoved. There were some few pleasures she would not deny herself.

'Kay! I've found it I tell you. We can go now.'

'Have you,' she murmured, still admiring the tall, dark-haired man, the small blond girl. They made a good couple, an interesting couple. And if *she* wondered about them, then everybody else would, too. She was relieved to have perceived the principle behind cover design. There was still a great deal for her to learn, after all.

'Kay!'

That time Sam spoke in his authoritarian voice, the one long cultivated, she was certain, out of bitter necessity. Sam was a widower, the father of three teenage hellions. Thinking of them, she was suddenly quite sorry for him.

She gave him a quick, reluctant glance, and saw the exact moment when he realized what she had been staring at. She knew that he couldn't have guessed why, nor what it meant to her, but he certainly realized that she had been looking slyly at the cover of a novel called *Adventuring*, the third book by a writer known as Chuck Lane.

The Hot Stars had been Chuck Lane's first. *Loving* had been his second. Peculiarly, all three seemed to appear wherever paperback books were sold. Their covers, always bright and provocative, leaped out at her from dozens of others in supermarkets, drugstores, department stores, bus stations. She never failed to study them with joy. *Adventuring* was still her favourite. It was the last one out. *Doing It* would be the next, and would, experience had already taught her, be her favourite for a little while.

But there was still Sam Golden. Whatever he realized, or guessed, or knew, his plump face turned red. His blue eyes narrowed with an emotion akin to pain, narrowed and peered at her from behind his black horn-rim glasses. 'Good heavens, Kay, dear,' he gasped. 'I only wanted to pick up a copy of *Life*. That story about Wall Street changes, you know. Very interesting stuff, I understand. But I never, truly, I never meant to expose you to that...to that vile...that vile junk!'

'Junk?' she asked tranquilly, giving the Chuck Lane by-line a last pleased look before she allowed Sam to nudge her away from the rack, and out of the store. 'Junk, Sam? Have you ever read any?'

It was really a well-designed cover, she was thinking. Of course, the by-line,

Chuck Lane, could have been a bit larger. But still...

'Read any of what?' Sam sputtered.

'Read any of Chuck Lane's books, Sam.' Her voice was full of its usual tranquillity, but she felt a thick hot wave of temper begin to rise in her. It matched the heat of the concrete sidewalk, the sun-glaring shop windows, the steaming parking lot.

She was red-headed, and appropriately spirited. But she had known as much argument, as much contention, as much screaming, fuming, articulate temper, as she cared to know. She had determined, five years before, at the time of her divorce from Earl Barrenger, that she would henceforth be amused, *coolly* amused, and *coolly* amused she was. Though sometimes, as when she walked with Sam across the parking lot, she thought she might choke on it.

Sam sounded as if he might be choking, too. 'Me? Read that guy's books? What do you think I am, Kay?'

'I don't know. But if you haven't read any of them, then you can't talk about them sensibly. You just don't know. And that's about all you can say.' It seemed to her a reasonable, a temperate remark.

But Sam exploded, 'I don't know that I have to read them to be certain of what they are. Junk! That's the only polite thing to call books like that. Just plain junk. Didn't you see the cover? Of course, you must have. You...'

'You sound awfully hot under the collar about it, Sam.'

'Well, good heavens, how would any decent person sound? The man who writes that stuff, what did you say his name was? Chuck Lane? Well, that man belongs in jail. And the publishers, the people who sell it, they belong in jail with him!'

Sam's plump face was scalding magenta. His usually mild blue eyes burned with moral fervour. His sloping shoulders squared, and his rounded waistline flattened. He plainly saw himself a crusader, going out to do battle with evil. The evil of the printed word.

Kay saw a rather ridiculous thirty-eight-year-old man in a conservative dark suit, a white shirt, a grey tie, sweating profusely in the heat of a humid August still-sunny twilight. She averted her amber eyes.

'In jail,' he repeated.

'Do you really think so, Sam?'

'I just said so!' He suddenly gave her a

suspicious stare. 'What's the matter with you, Kay? Don't tell me you waste your time on that—that garbage. Truly, don't tell me that, Kay, dear, you mustn't tell me that you've read those books by Chuck Lane, or whatever he calls himself.'

The thick hot wave of temper against which she had been struggling miraculously melted away. Her amber eyes suddenly glowed with real amusement. 'All right, Sam,' she said. 'I won't tell you that.'

By then, they had crossed the shopping centre parking lot, wended careful paths through ranks of improperly-angled cars, and reached Sam's conservative grey Buick.

He helped her in, closed the door, went around to the driver's side, and got in behind the wheel. He cleaned his black horn-rim glasses carefully with a white linen handkerchief that was as large as a sheet, then mopped the dew of indignation, plus the dew of an eastern seaboard August, from his round cheeks.

Kay assumed that the subject was closed, and sat back with a sigh of relief.

She was a small girl, curved in the right places, but small just the same. She had tiny, high-arched feet, and always wore spike heels when dressed up, fruitlessly

16

seeking the extra inch that she would have considered a barely adequate height, had she been given it. Her red hair, shot through with gold, was cut short, and curled in unobtrusive bangs across her wide forehead. In spite of her red hair, and the temper that matched it, her curved pink lips were set in a careful smile most of the time. Her firm chin was held at a meek angle. It was held at so meek an angle that many people saw the dimple rather than the strength. An error she regularly encouraged, and silently enjoyed.

She and Sam were going to dinner at the Devlins', friends, neighbours, and cohorts. So Kay was wearing a lettuce-green shift, cut high at the throat, and sleeveless, and pumps dyed to match, and crumpled somewhere inside her lettuce-green purse was a pair of lettuce-green gloves.

It was necessary, since Sandra Devlin and Kay's mother, Amanda Mason, were very good friends, in spite of something like a fifteen-year age difference, to present an especially good appearance. Otherwise Sandra, who regularly conferred with Amanda about Kay, would give an unsatisfactory report, and in the morning, come hell, high water, or howling winds, perhaps even before coffee, Kay would have to listen to Amanda give forth.

Amanda gave forth beautifully. But Kay was twenty-six. She had been divorced for five years, after two years of marriage. She had Donnie, who was six years old, all boy and a yard and a half high. She had her own home, and was dependent on no one. She was tranquil, amused, competent, and involved in more projects than she cared to think of at any one time. Also involved in more projects than she cared to discuss at any series of times. Yet all of Greenhill eyed her with suspicion, concern, and dismay. Amanda, Sandra, the rest of them, would not be content until Kay was paired off with somebody. With anybody. As long as he was male. Hence Sam Golden.

Kay sighed again. At least he had forgotten about Chuck Lane.

But as Sam backed out of the parking lot, sheet-sized handkerchief restored to his pocket, glasses replaced firmly on his nose, he said, 'Kay, truly, that is an area in which I think you might profitably interest yourself. After all, there's my three boys...now suppose they got hold of that stuff...'

18

Kay considered a number of replies, and ended up saying nothing. She was pretty sure that Chuck Lane couldn't teach even the youngest of Sam's boys a thing.

'All right, never mind my boys,' Sam went on, after a moment's silence. 'But there *is* Donnie. And how would you feel...'

Kay ignored the oblique reproach. She said as little as possible, she even thought as little as possible, about Sam's three sons. Amanda, without learning the lesson she preached, had long before taught Katy that if one could say nothing nice about people, it was best to say nothing at all. Now Kay told Sam brightly, 'Oh, Donnie? I'm going to tell him.'

'What?'

'I'm going to tell him. He's bored with birds and bees. He's finished with flowers. So—'

'How would you feel...' Sam repeated firmly, 'if Donnie were to...'

'What?'

'Now, Kay, I've been thinking. And what you could do...'

'What?'

'Sure, Kay. You.'

'What?' she asked again.

19

'It's a natural for you, too. Give you something to do. An interest in life. And, of course, after all, you're on the P.T.A committees already, aren't you? You do a lot of work for them anyway, and you've earned the wonderful reputation for getting things done. You ought to start a campaign. See to ways and means of getting that stuff off the shelves, out of the stores, unsold and unseen. That's the ticket. Yes, yes, truly, that's it. And just suppose Donnie, your own little boy that's so dear to your heart...'

'But, Sam...'

'I'm a firm believer in the power of a woman, you know. Get the women interested, Kay. And there won't be any more dirty books. Believe me, you can do it. If you only had the confidence in yourself that I have in you. You can do it, Kay. If you want to.' He went on enthusiastically in the face of her unenthusiastic silence, 'It might spread all over the country. Imagine Kay, headlines...yes, of course, headlines. Greenhill woman sparks sex book clean-up!'

Kay swallowed a wave of nausea that was followed by a wave of mirth. She leaned her head against the window frame, allowed the hot wet wind to touch her bangs. At last, she said carefully. 'There are people who are supposed to handle things like that, Sam. I mean...you know...the sheriffs, the courts...specialists...'

'Street action, direct action,' Sam said vigorously. 'The people speak! That's what it really takes. Not sheriffs, not courts, not specialists. Direct action, in the streets—'

'Barricades and bonfires,' Kay murmured.

Sam gave her a narrow blue look. 'What's that, Kay?'

'Nothing.'

'But you did say...'

'You're talking in slogans, Sam. All caps.'

'That's it.' He looked pleased. 'Slogans. Make the world safe for our kids. Get the garbage off the bookstands.'

'Sam...'

'Say, that's pretty good. Get the garbage off our bookstands.'

'Outlaw sex.'

'What?'

'Nothing, Sam.'

'Sex?' He turned, grinned. 'Now you're talking. Sex. Yes. I've been trying to tell you for months...'

'Sam,' she said gently, 'Sam, did you ever—'

21

'That's just what I've been trying to work up to for months. Listen, Kay. We don't have to stay long at the Devlins. Just say you're worried about Donnie. Say...'

'We're talking about books,' Kay told him. 'Remember? The paperback books. Now, did you ever....?'

He cut in, 'Of course not. I told you. I never read the stuff. I don't have time.'

'Then, Sam,' she said gently. 'You just don't know what you're talking about, do you?'

He didn't seem to hear her. A plump hand dropped from the steering wheel to clasp the cotton of her skirt, to smooth the curve of her thigh. 'Yes, that's a wonderful idea. We'll leave early. We'll find a place. As a matter of fact...just trust me, Kay. I've been around. I happen to know just the...'

She said gently, as she wriggled away, 'Stop it, Sam.'

His hand immediately returned to the steering wheel. His magenta face went from dreamy anticipation to stern duty. 'If you get the women interested, then you'll...'

She thought that maybe, Sam, one of those days. But no, he simply was not the stuff from which heroes were made. Not her heroes anyhow. If there had been anything in those quick pawing sessions, she hadn't noticed it. She sighed. Yes, he was definitely back on the books again.

'...then...listen, Kay, really, it's a natural for you, for the kind of woman you are.'

'Me? You really mean me, Sam?'

'Of course. Why not, Kay?'

There were several different reasons why not. She thought of them, listed them, smiled over them, and then she said only, 'Oh, I couldn't. I hate crusades. And besides, I'm just too busy.'

'Too busy to save your sons? My sons?'

'My son,' she said. 'Singular, Sam. My son.' Then, 'Save him from what?'

'Those books. Those covers. That garbage... that...'

'Sam...' her voice was still gentle. 'Listen, Sam, you propositioned me a little while ago. Remember?'

He grunted.

'Well, you did, you know. And you know just about everything that goes on in Greenhill, too, don't you?'

He grunted again.

She went on, 'What do you think is in

23

those paperbacks, Sam?'

'The covers—'

'You can't just judge a book—'

He groaned. 'Cliches, Kay?'

She smiled at him. 'Remember, Sam?' And she quoted. ' "We can leave early. We can find a place..." '

He groaned again.

She could have gone on to prove the point. She could have mentioned her father's mistress, Sweet Cynthia, and Amanda's string of decidedly too-young lovers, and...

Instead, she let it go. She smoothed her red-gold curls and thought that it was really too bad.

Sam certainly wasn't the worst man in the world. Of that, she was certain.

She had been married to the worst one, and had seen her marriage end with more relief than regret. No one, not friend, nor family, seemed willing to accept that. But it was the truth. She had married Earl at nineteen. She was a junior in college; he was a senior then. Within the few breathless months between the day they met and the day they married, he swept her from the dreamy expectations of late adolescence to the peaks and troughs of

24

passion, and then very soon, to the tunnels of despair.

She was too young then to know that any man with the capacity for so much torrid romance in his soul could never be satisfied with one girl. He was too young then to know it himself.

The tunnels of despair... It had begun with a passing fancy on their honeymoon. Earl, on the golf course and...it had shocked Kay. She remained shocked through the next two years. Earl just couldn't stop chasing women, falling in love with them, bedding them down, forgetting them. He won Kay for his wife. He proceeded on to the next conquest. He had a son. He proceeded on to the next conquest.

Kay divorced him. She supposed he had gone on in the same way. She took Donnie and went home. She stayed there a week. Her father gave her the money for a house three blocks away in Greenhill. It made him nervous, she suspected, to have his wife, his daughter, his grandson, around, while he pursued Sweet Cynthia on Tuesdays and Thursdays.

Kay gratefully settled into her new home. She didn't have much, but it was enough. She finished her last two years of college.

She took care of Donnie. The two of them prospered. But now, after five years, Amanda, a youngish country club type at forty-four, still couldn't believe that no man was better than the wrong one. So Sam Golden, and his three teenage terrors, had been rung into the scene. But Kay had finally decided, even if Amanda, and Donnie, both liked Sam, he was as much the wrong man for Kay as Earl Barrenger had been. On balance, now that she considered it, she thought that she might even prefer Earl Barrenger.

Relieved that another worrisome decision had been neatly and completely, taken out of her hands, she widened her amber eyes and smiled. Goodbye, Sam.

He, oblivious to her thoughts, accused her in tones of ragged patience, 'Kay, I don't think you're listening to me.'

She answered in tones of honeyed patience, 'What, Sam?'

'I was talking about those books.'

'Again?'

'I don't understand you, Kay.'

She gave him a flash of amber eyes. 'You don't?'

'Anyone would think...'

'You know,' she cut in, 'I think I've

considered those books that upset you so much just as much as I want to consider them, Sam. Maybe even more than I want to.' Seeing that his plump face had suddenly developed intense lines, which meant that he was about to argue, browbeat, contend, or instruct, she sought wildly for a diversion, and found it in the middle of the block ahead. She carolled, 'Oh, look, Sam, we're here. At the Devlins' already!'

'We're late,' he said gloomily. But the intense lines dissolved. He slowed at the intersection, eased the big Buick to the curb before a long, low, white, stucco house.

It was surrounded by hydrangeas the same blue as the blue twilight. For a moment, Kay wondered if Sandra Devlin had dyed the bushes, or could she have dyed the twilight? to achieve that particularly impressive effect.

'I wanted to talk to you,' Sam said heavily. 'I mean it, Kay. I have something on my mind.'

'You do?' She dismissed Sandra's quite unique ability to achieve effects, some for good, some for ill, and tried very hard to concentrate on Sam. She believed that he deserved at least that much. Maybe.

'Amanda, your mother, I mean, she asked me to call her that. Amanda, you know. Well, she and I...we've been worrying about you, Kay. You don't seem to be getting anywhere. To be doing anything. I mean...of course, you do hide it well, and we both realize that, and we're proud of you for it, too, but you're not happy. You're not fulfilled. Not as you could be. And we understand. Amanda and I, we're both grownups. Just as you are, of course...don't think I mean...but anyway, we would want—'

Kay wondered briefly how she would feel about Sam as a stepfather. Perhaps James could be induced to divorce Amanda, to marry Sweet Cynthia. Then Sam and Amanda, while discussing poor Kay's joyless, manless, empty life, might...But no. It just wouldn't do. James didn't want to divorce Amanda to marry Sweet Cynthia. He couldn't bear her for more than Tuesdays and Thursdays. Kay snapped the car door open, and thought once more, Goodbye, Sam.

He cut his stammers short. He leaped out, hurried around just in time to brush her elbow as she jumped the curb, a puddle, a beach ball, to land in soaking-wet grass. She muttered her thanks, hoping that green stains wouldn't show too much on lettuce-green shoes, and dodged around him to get to the Devlin door.

It was pale yellow, bracketed in brass. A brass imp leered at her from the clapper. She hit the imp hard; it croaked. The door swung open.

Sandra Devlin stood there, framed like a breathing portrait, and posed like a breathing portrait. Her hair was dark, long, and fell to her shoulders in unfashionable waves. Her face was a smooth oval, black eyes accentuated by sooty lashes, eye-liner, mascara; crooked smile accentuated by pure, clear shiny red.

She wore a long white at-home skirt, a scarlet top. Her country club tan spread like a film of dull satin on her bare shoulders and throat, and into the deep cleft of her halter.

'You're just in time,' she said, 'Michael is mixing the first of the evening. So come on in.'

'Sam was afraid we were late,' Kay answered, following her into the house. And thought that Sandra's dark slanted eyes seemed full of secrets, and her lush mouth, painted to match the scarlet halter... Kay cut it off there. She told herself firmly to quit thinking like Chuck Lane.

Michael Devlin grinned at her across the expanse of living room.

It was of teak, marble, indoor plants, a Yugoslavian rug, glass walls well-draped for privacy. A typical Greenhill house, just as the Devlins were a typical Greenhill couple.

Kay considered that and decided to remember it.

'Scotch and soda okay for you, Kay?' Michael was asking. 'What about you, Sam? Or are you going to insist on being pure pure pure and demand Martinis before dinner?'

'What kind of Scotch?' Sam demanded.

Kay resisted an urge to kick him.

But Michael laughed. 'Guess.'

He was tall, with close-cropped blond hair, a square pleasant face that was well-tanned from golf sessions. He had blue eyes set in a maze of smile lines, and laughed a great deal, yet Kay had noticed before that those blue eyes of his never smiled. He was a successful attorney, the Devlin of Aker and Devlin. Aker was his father-in-law.

A typical Greenhill house, Kay thought again, and eyed Michael and Sandra. Yes. And a typical Greenhill couple, too.

Sandra said throatily. 'Why, Sam, are you being difficult? I never guessed you were an expert on Scotch?'

He looked pleased, a flush on his plump cheeks, but didn't answer.

Kay moaned silently. She had developed a sudden ache under her red-gold curls. Her amber eyes stung. Her small feet itched to be up and away.

It might have been all right if Sam hadn't, after accepting his drink, sipping it, rolling it obviously around his tongue, if he hadn't then pointedly omitted a compliment to Michael on his taste in Scotch. It might have been all right if Sam hadn't then dedicated himself to making conversation where none was necessary.

He said, 'On the way over, and it's why we were late, really, I stopped at that newsstand in the shopping centre. I wanted a copy of *Life*. There's that spread about changes on Wall Street. I like to keep up, you know.'

'You needn't have bought it,' Sandra told him. 'We have it. It's right there on the table. You could have had it if you

31

were interested, and saved yourself the...'

'Well, I am, as I said, so I did,' Sam said.

It was of such suggested small economies, Kay reminded herself, that great fortunes were made. Her eyes sought Sandra. What did that tall, slim, dark-eyed nymph know of such economies?

Chuck Lane again. Once more Kay told herself to quit.

'But while I was there,' Sam was saying, 'that's the point of what I wanted to tell you, while I was there, looking for *Life*, Kay and I noticed some books. Books! I don't know what to call them actually. But the covers...! You just can't imagine those covers!'

Michael chuckled. 'You sound like Rip van Winkle. Where the hell have you been the last twenty years anyway?'

'Hush, Michael.' That was Sandra, throaty, interested, and up to no good. And to Sam, 'What covers are you talking about?'

Michael said, 'You know what covers, Sandra girl.'

'Don't call me Sandra girl.' She turned her narrow dark eyes on him, examined him as if he were a type of six-legged

32

insect, then carefully looked away. 'What covers do you mean, Sam?'

'Paperbacks,' Kay told her. 'You know... the usual pictures. Men. Women..'

'Some guy named Chuck Lane. It seems to me I know that guy,' Sam said. 'I've heard about him before somewhere.'

Kay laughed. 'Maybe you *have* read his books after all.'

Sam said stiffly, 'Kay, really, I can't think why you consider this to be funny. I'm serious. Dead serious.'

'I know you are,' she said, and laughed again.

Sandra asked, 'Serious about what, Sam?'

'Those books. What do you think? I was telling Kay she ought to do something about them. Get them off the bookstands, get them out of town, out of the state. Suppose our kids read them. Suppose...'

Sandra hitched her halter a bit lower, and leaned forward, giving Kay, and Sam, a clear view of tanned curves, and Michael a clear view of one expressive shoulder. In her most sultry voice, Sandra purred 'Why, Sam, those books must be just awful. Are they hard-core pornography? Under the counter stuff? And what were you doing under the counter?'

'I wasn't. They were on the stands, where anybody could see them. Books. A bunch of them. By Chuck Lane, and...'

'Oh,' Sandra seemed to melt with disappointment, 'not hard-core then. Just plain ordinary paperbacks, about plain ordinary people, and plain ordinary sex. And selling for sixty cents a shot. Is that what you mean?'

'Garbage,' Sam growled.

'Why, Sam! Are you a censor? A bookburner? Are you against real Americanism?'

'Of course not! What are you talking about? I'm telling you that that garbage ought to—'

Sandra purred, 'Well, maybe, maybe. And maybe I wouldn't have it, or anything like it in my house, but...but who are you, Sam? Who am I? Can we decide what other people will read?'

'Not you. Not me,' Sam said firmly. 'I think Kay should do it. Yes, that's right, Kay. She's exactly the right person. She can work through the P.T.A, head a committee, get people interested. In no time at all...'

Sandra gave Kay a sidelong look. 'I do

believe you're right, Sam. If Kay put her mind to it—'

Kay found her small green purse and surged to her feet. 'Be right back,' she mumbled, and fled into the foyer.

'Fresh towel in the powder room cabinet as usual,' Sandra purred.

Kay let the hot water run loud and long. It made nice satisfying splash marks on the powder room carpet, splashes that turned purple as they soaked into the lavender pile. She opened the lavender formica cabinet under the lavender sink, and jerked out a lavender towel.

Something came with it. Something that made a muffled thud on the splash-stained rug.

She looked down, grinned.

Adventuring by Chuck Lane.

Yes, she decided, it was a nice cover. Really quite well-designed. Perhaps the "Chuck Lane" could be a bit larger, but still...

She carefully replaced *Adventuring* in the cache from which it had come. She buried it so neatly that no corner showed from within the stack of lavender towels.

She ran a quick comb through her curls, sketched a deeper pink bow on her mouth.

She decided that Sandra would bear some watching. *Adventuring* hidden in the towels of the powder room. Now why? Yes, Sandra would bear some watching. Or, thinking back, Kay suddenly asked herself if Sandra could possibly be watching her?

Back in the living room, Kay found Sandra still expounding throatily, while Michael mixed a fresh round of drinks, and Sam polished his glasses.

Kay sighed. She sneaked a glance at her wristwatch. She wondered if dinner were imminent. She wondered if there would be dinner at all. She, unlike the others, had a long night ahead of her.

A second round, a third. Kay accepted it, but didn't drink. The last was two too many. At last, wistfully, she said, 'You know what? I'm starved.'

Sandra reluctantly forbade Michael the fourth round he had obviously been planning, and led the way into the dining room.

It was over char-broiled steak and duchesse potatoes that Sam reverted to an earlier, and as far as Kay was concerned, a worn-out topic. He leaned forward to peer earnestly at the cleft in Sandra's halter. 'Really, Sandra, you ought to talk to Kay.

I mean, really talk to her.'

Kay moaned silently.

Sandra said, 'You mean really talk to her? About what?'

'About doing something.'

'Doing something about Chuck Lane?' Michael demanded.

'That, yes, of course, I said so before,' Sam said stiffly, plainly avoiding the warning look Kay sent him. 'But, well, if not that, then anything. She stays in too much. She needs...well, we're adults here, aren't we? She needs diversion, attention, and...'

'Love?' Michael suggested.

'Will you provide it?' Sandra asked sweetly.

It wasn't completely clear whether the question was directed at Michael, or at Sam. But Sam's plump face turned magenta. He hauled out his sheet-size handkerchief and mopped carefully, and then, just as carefully, he folded and tucked the handkerchief away. Michael meanwhile, nonchalantly chewed char-broiled steak.

Kay listened to the brief meaningful silence, and smiled emptily, thinking of what she would do when she finally got home. If she ever survived to get home.

At last, with no help from anyone, Sam struggled manfully with his embarrassment, and conquered it, to say. 'I've been doing the best I can, of course. But *I* wasn't talking about *that.*'

'About *that?*' Michael repeated, laughing softly.

'But what else is there?' Sandra cried.

Kay, with a perfectly straight face, said, 'I really do a lot, Sam. I'm secretary of the League of Women Voters. I'm secretary-treasurer of the Little League. I'm treasurer of the Flower Club. I sew for the Thespians. Somebody from PWP, that's Parents Without Partners to you, keeps harassing me to join, and I wonder who the devil gave them my name. It seems to me that...'

'But Amanda says...'

Sandra put in, 'With all due respect to your mother, Kay, we both know that Amanda goes to the beauty parlour three times a week, and to the country club. And that's all that she does. So...'

Kay grinned gratefully at Sandra, unaccustomed to having an ally.

Sandra purred, 'And Kay practices her typing, too.'

Kay stopped grinning.

Michael laughed, the smile lines at his blue eyes deepening, the eyes themselves completely untouched by warmth. 'You're getting to be our regular little problem child, aren't you, Kay?'

She answered in a light voice. 'It seems so. But unwillingly.'

Under the table, a hand reached for her knee, groped at her thigh. She glanced at Sandra, shifted her position. The hand fell away.

'Unwillingly,' she repeated, and Michael laughed again.

It was a breathless, starless, moonless night.

The Buick, coasting through the dark, was like a ship on a shadowed sea.

Sam was a silent, stern captain.

Kay was a silent, preoccupied passsenger, relieved, finally, to reach the safety of land. That is to say, of her front door.

With his hand on hers, Sam asked, 'Couldn't I come in for a minute, Kay? I did really want to talk to you.'

'Some other time,' Kay told him. 'It's late, and I'm tired, and I have some things I want to do.'

'You always say that, but I'll be damned,

oh, excuse me, Kay, but that's just what I mean, I'll be damned if I can see what you do.'

She didn't answer him.

'I'm sorry, Kay.'

She grinned at him.

'But, just the same, Amanda's right.'

'You're not going to start that again, are you?'

He looked bewildered. 'What do you mean?'

'About Amanda.'

'Not about Amanda, oh, no. I mean, I think your mother's just fine, but what I wanted...'

Kay cut in firmly, 'Sorry. Not now.'

His hand slipped from hers. He made a quick ineffectual grab at her waist, and thrust his face down at hers.

She ducked and twirled, crying, 'Thanks for everything. I have to go in. Goodbye, Sam,' and closed the door on his muted sputter.

She leaned there, and thought that it really was too bad.

She supposed Amanda was right.

There really ought to be a man, some men, in the life of a twenty-six-year-old woman.

40

Then Lee Berg, the baby-sitter, fifteen, wide-eyed, acne-marked, and narrow-shouldered, loped into the front hall. 'That you, Mrs Barrenger?'

'It's me, Lee. Who were you expecting?'

'You. Who else would I be expecting?'

'That's what I mean, Lee.'

'What?'

She said carefully. 'If you were expecting me, then why did you ask if it was me?'

'What?'

She looked at him helplessly. 'Never mind, Lee. It's not important.'

'But, say, listen, Mrs Barrenger—'

'Never mind.'

'Anyhow,' he said after a long silent moment, 'Anyhow, there wasn't a peep out of Donnie.'

'Good.' She paid Lee quickly, saw him off with relief.

There were, after all, some men in her life. Lee, Donnie.

She locked up, put on tailored blue pyjamas. She brushed her teeth, which was pleasant, and her hair which was relaxing. She took cigarettes, and went into the kitchen.

It was her favourite room. While the rest of the house was old, and showed it, the kitchen was brand-span new, a bare three months old, and showed it, too.

There was a huge window, shelved to show off the coloured glass vases she had begun collecting when she was a child. Before Amanda started with her too-young men, and James started with his Sweet Cynthia. There was a huge round wooden work table. A yellow formica counter, set at just the right height. A perfect walk-in pantry. A huge sun-yellow refrigerator waited stodgily in one corner. A big sun-yellow stove filled another. The walls were white, hung with black-framed prints of world capitals. Three quick glances took her from London, to Paris, to Rome. Two more took her from Athens to Budapest.

She stood in the doorway, looking at her favourite room, and forgot Sam, and Sandra and Michael.

She smiled at the white walls the yellow appliances. She went into the pantry, and brought back with her her portable typewriter, and set it on the counter top. She adjusted ashtrays, cigarettes, pencils and erasers into a predestined order.

Then, still smiling, she pulled a chair close to the yellow refrigerator. She climbed up and slowly edged the huge cookie bin to within fingertip grasp.

It was a particularly large one, surely ten inches deep, and fifteen inches long and wide. It was painted dark brown, and lined with yellow, so that it seemed, at a quick glance, to look like a treasure chest.

She inched the dented top open, and reached inside it, groping because she couldn't see. From within, she took a thick stack of yellow paper. She pressed the lid of the cookie bin shut, and climbed down from the chair.

Yellow stack of paper in hand, she settled at the counter.

The straight copying was what she hated most. Two hundred pages to be typed, to be corrected. But hated or not, it had to be done.

She fitted white paper, carbon, yellow copy sheet, together, and slipped them into the portable. Her fingers hit the keys. After a moment, she paused to look at what she had written.

Doing It
by
Kay Barrenger

She swore, and tore the pages out. She

43

ripped them into careful shreds, stacked the shreds neatly next to the ashtray. She fitted more pages together, put them into the machine, and began again, watching the words appear as she typed them.

Doing It
by
Chuck Lane

Chapter 1.

She went ahead, smiling.
Chuck Lane's fourth book.
Her fourth book.
Chuck Lane was the man in her life.

CHAPTER 2

Hello, Sex

It all started with a series of small events. Without those small events, none of them world-shaking, nor even particularly meaningful, none of it would have happened.

It was the spring of the year before, and

Kay had come down with a virulent case of the seasonal disease. Robins trilled sharp and sweet in the blooming lilacs. Cardinals sang in the misty weeping willow.

Then fat Mr Fairbanks came waddling up the walk to deliver the mail earlier than usual.

And then Amanda had called to deliver the usual lecture.

It was thus that, instead of proceeding to basement and laundry after scrubbing the kitchen floor that never looked clean, Kay proceeded, in a small act of rebellion, to sit down for a second cup of coffee. While she drank it, savouring the thick, slightly sour taste, she flipped the pages of the writers' magazine to which, in another small act of rebellion, she had subscribed months before.

The advertisement, two inches square and bordered in grey, caught her eye. Mostly because within that grey border was some bold print which suggested that anybody could use FIFTEEN HUNDRED DOLLARS.

Kay had already spent the fifteen hundred before she read the fine print below.

Britanica Company, Inc. writers' agents,

is in the market for novels, forty thousand words long, racy, with vitality, life, reality, about real men and women for adult men and women.

Kay read the advertisement twice, and worked out the necessary translation. *Racy* meant sexy. *Vitality* meant virility. *Life* meant trouble. *Reality* meant a happy ending after all. *About real men and women for adult men and women* simply meant sex again.

The translation completed to her satisfaction, she decided that she was all for Britanica Company, Inc., for their New York post office box number, for their "write for information" to Galen Maradick, for their FIFTEEN HUNDRED DOLLARS.

Not that she had any illusions. Fifteen hundred dollars did not linger in New York post office boxes simply waiting for young innocents to come along with eagerly outthrust hands. And she didn't suppose that the putting down of forty thousand consecutive words in an order that made sense was something that would happen with miraculous ease.

But, and it was a very big *but* indeed, she knew the subject. She knew it even better than she cared to. She had put in two over-full years with Earl. She had, at the time of reading the advertisement, already put in four overfull years as a young, red-headed divorcee. She was, even then, doing a weak Australian crawl through the cesspool known as Greenhill. What with James and Amanda for parents, Earl as an ex-husband, an assortment of happily forgotten swains, Kay had something to say about real men and real women, and she was certain that what she didn't know she could easily imagine.

She never read the rest of the magazine. She never did the laundry that day. Instead she calculated how many pages she would have to fill on her portable to add up to forty thousand words. Roughly two hundred pages. Which had a considerably more possible sound to it than forty thousand words.

She wrote a brief note to Britanica Company, Inc., attention: Mr Galen Maradick, asking for further information, and signed it with her own name. After thinking it over, she retyped that same brief note and signed it, with a grim smile, "Mrs Earl Barrenger." She went out to mail it immediately, and on the way back, she stopped for a ream of yellow paper, a thick stack of envelopes, typewriter ribbon, cleaner, and eraser. An unexamined impulse led her to pop into the drugstore for a look at the paperback display. She had whiled away many bored, lonely, sleepless, anguish-filled nights with mysteries. This time she avoided them. She chose three books from that large group of which cover and blurb suggested she would find what she sought: a clue as to how to get started.

'And how are you this beautiful spring morning?' Mr Avis, the drugstore owner, asked her, while she fished in her purse.

He was a plump old man, full of beer, and high colour, with a round bald head that was as pink as a newly-polished apple. He loved to talk, and since the chain drugstore had opened up in the shopping centre down the road, a stop to pick up a bottle of aspirin had become a social visit with him.

Now, as he accepted the books from Kay, looked down to check their prices, he went on, 'A beautiful spring morning, and you with time on your hands, hunh? All this reading material. My, my, a pretty girl like you...' His plump face suddenly broke into a wide grin. 'This here, it's a good one.' He caressed a shiny yellow cover. 'Yes, indeedy, a hot one all right.' He raised knowing brown eyes. 'You're a picker, all right. Only a pretty girl like you...'

She hurriedly thrust two dollars into his plump pink hand, wondering if she imagined that his fingers had brushed hers for just that instant too long that made the difference between accident and purpose. She said witlessly, 'It's a lovely morning, isn't it?' and accepted the change he gave her, and as she fled, she crammed the books into the big stationers' bag, where they nestled against the ream of yellow paper she had bought.

Back in her kitchen, with a fresh cup of coffee poured, and a cigarette lit, she settled into the rickety chair, to examine what old Mr Avis had so highly recommended. She forgot to drink, to smoke. Fascinated, she read. Fascinated, she flipped the pages. Her eyebrows rose; her lips pursed in a silent whistle.

The pulsations in her body became unbearable just about, and she shifted to the rim of the chair. She pressed her weight downward, hard, thrusting. She hoped that moment would ease the cresting current that was so quickly becoming beyond control. That movement, though, served only to stir, to strengthen, to build, her hunger.

'For goodness sakes,' Kay said, and didn't know she was speaking aloud, 'That must have been written by a man.'
She flipped pages, stopped to read the end of a chapter.

Being unmarried, Ran Jones considered himself completely qualified to read the look on a girl's face. Especially when it gave the idea that she had either just come to a quivering climax, or was hopefully imagining that she was being loved up, down and around, until she made it.

'Well,' Kay said, still unaware that she was speaking aloud, 'What a very moral man, or one with an odd opinion of husbands..."being unmarried," Ran Jones considered himself completely qualified...'
She closed and set aside the book with the shiny yellow cover. Old Mr Avis' recommendation was not her style at all.
She considered a quick scanning of the

other two books she had gotten, then decided that no, she would be better off to go her own way.

She lit a fresh cigarette, sipped cold coffee, and ~~dove~~ *dived* head first into her own fantasies.

The Hot Stars.

She liked that, but didn't pause too long to admire it.

Chapter 1.

She liked that, too, but with a long, deep breath, she went ahead.

Earl said softly, 'What do you know about love?' His deep probing kiss smothered her shy whisper. His hands stroking insistently at her breast, strangely exciting, made her forget what she had been going to say, and it didn't matter. She didn't have to say anything. Her long taut body, lifting to his was answer enough. His mouth parted from hers for a moment. She felt the chill of air on her breasts, then the heat of his face as his lips tongued her left nipple until it tightened, coarsened, rose up. A hundred quick arrows of excitement flicked through her. Her fingers, caressing his cheeks, urged his lips to her right breast, and he settled there, for a moment, licking gently. His hands moved down, shaping her hips and tracing the length of her thighs. Warm insinuating fingers moved between them, trailing humid heat. Her legs opened slightly, and her hips came up. She gasped, 'Show me, Earl. Show me about love.'

And that was a good enough beginning for Kay.

By the time Donnie had come home from kindergarten, she had five pages written. They steamed all over the kitchen table, a rickety insubstantial thing, while Earl taught Bonnie what he thought she ought to know. Those five pages steamed so much that Kay found herself blushing.

She had made the translation, come up with SEX. She had five pages full of SEX, and a couple of notes that might go into a plot.

Two days later, Mr Fairbanks wheezed up the walk, to squint at her. 'You don't hardly ever get letters addressed like this, you don't.'

She snatched it out of his hand.

Yes. Britanica Company, Inc., attention: Mr Galen Maradick, had answered her query.

She ignored Mr Fairbanks' comments about the spring day, the desperate need for spring rain, the plight of his onion garden. She grinned and gabbled nonsense words and ducked inside.

Britanica Company, Inc, wrote a nice form letter, one full page in mimeograph-formed words. Under a really impressive letterhead, it told her that it would be delighted to hear further from her. It said happily that it would read a synopsis (outline) and maybe thirty pages of text (part of the novel), or it would read a full-length novel. That was up to her. The fact that she might prefer to try her idea out in the short form first would in no way militate against her in the judgement of her work. If acceptable, it would deduct ten percent of the selling price, provided the publisher paid for it. If it could not handle her work because she was not quite ready for selling, but showed signs of promise, it could joyfully offer its teaching services and advice. 'Let us hear from you,' Kay quoted happily to herself.

Britanica Company. Inc., attention: Galen Maradick, wanted sample text and synopsis. For fifteen hundred dollars (*possibly,* Kay underscored to herself) they could have them.

She typed, retyped, daydreamed, swore some, and within three days, she stuffed what she had done, between giving Donnie milk and peanut butter sandwiches after school, and giving Donnie hamburger at dinner time, and seeing to toothbrushing, and pyjamas, and prayers, and answering umpteen telephone calls, and begging off from the P.T.A meeting she had forgotten, after all that, and the typing, daydreaming, and swearing, she stuffed what she had done into a big envelope, and made a rough guess at the postage, and started out for the corner mail box.

On the way, breathing the sweet spring air, she thought of the next one. *Loving. Chapter 1. He was a tall man, and moved with a long lithe stride. He came swiftly around the corner. The small girl standing there cried, 'Oh, Earl...' He...*

Kay crossed to the mail box. With the envelope halfway down its red maw, she jerked it back. She felt suddenly as if she had been standing at the edge of a cliff, with one foot dangling dangerously in empty air.

Suppose Britanica Company, Inc. could sell *The Hot Stars?* Improbably as it seemed, just suppose that. She would get fifteen hundred dollars. The world would get a new paperback.

She imagined the cover on it. A man...Oh, yes. There was always a man on a paperback book cover. What would Amanda say? What would James say? What would...?

Kay devised a dozen quick fantasies.

Amanda would twitch her delicately-tilted nose, and smooth her carefully-set curls, and say, 'Now, really, Kay darling, this is all right. Of course it is. But it's only a substitute for living. That's all. Just a substitute. Cold comfort on cold nights. Now I know a very sweet young man...' And then, 'Besides, Kay, dear, what on earth will people think of you? What on earth will people say?'

James would study the book cover, if it was one of *those* books, and one of *those* covers, and tell her gently, 'Well, never mind, Kay, after all, you're not the artist. You didn't draw the stuff. You only wrote it, so...' but he would never look past the outside to the inside to see what she had written. Instead, he would study her with uneasy pity, mumble, 'I know you don't have much to do with your time, but...'

And the P.T.A? The Thespians?

Kay pulled herself out of the quick fantasies. She turned, walked slowly back to the house, clutching the envelope in sweaty fingers.

She was depressed, disgusted, discouraged, and worst of all, she was ashamed of herself.

She didn't even have the intestinal fortitude to do what she really wanted to do. She turned that phrase, intestinal fortitude, over in her mind, and decided, Damn that! I'm a writer! What I mean is guts. Why don't I think guts! say guts! I don't even have the plain ordinary guts to do what I want to do. Which is to put that synopsis, that little bit of hot sexy and truly written text, into the mail to Britanica Company, Inc.

That was what she wanted to do, all she wanted to do. That first. Then came *Loving, Chapter 1. He was a tall man, and moved...*

Instead, glumly, she stuffed the whole thing, envelope and all, into the huge ugly treasure chest cookie bin that squatted on top of the wheezing grey-white, chipped refrigerator that was too small even for such a small family as hers. She stuffed *The Hot Stars* into the cookie bin, and expected the metal cookie bin to melt.

It didn't. Disappointed, she turned away.

Amanda, James, the whole Greenhill crowd, were down on her. They had been ever since she divorced Earl, and came back with Donnie. She had rocked the boat. She had done what the rest of them wouldn't do. They didn't approve of her, of the way she lived. They didn't like the line she had drawn between herself and them.

James had given her the house, and that was all. He never asked if she needed money to manage on. She never told him that she did. Earl sent her a support cheque for Donnie, a sum based on standards set by prices in the Stone Age. She had managed, through the past four years, to make that inadequate amount do for two.

Amanda worried that there were no men in Kay's life, and trotted around whole series of easily-forgotten types, all second-hand Earls, in different shapes and sizes. James worried that she was becoming a dedicated suburbanite, with a weakness for unimportant causes. The rest of Greenhill, Sandra and Michael Devlin included, seemed worried only that they didn't know about the secret life they were certain in their hearts that she must live.

She could just imagine the faces they would all pull, the questions she would have to answer, the pressure she would have to endure, were they to come up on *The Hot Stars* by Kay Barrenger on the newsstand.

And what about plump old Mr Avis? His knowing, eager, brown eyes. She shuddered to think of the social visits at his cash register after he had read 'by Kay Barrenger' on his racks.

No. No. No. She didn't want any of that. Nor did she want any argument, any questions, and pressure. She...

She had turned away from the cookie bin. But she hadn't gone very far. Half a step later, she was back, salvaging *The Hot Stars,* what there was of them, she told herself. She was, even then, looking forward to finishing the book, to spending the fifteen hundred dollars, to beginning another book, to spending another fifteen hundred dollars.

If she couldn't use her own name, she reasoned, and she couldn't, there was Donnie, Amanda, James, to think about, then she could use someone else's name.

She was terribly, bitterly, tempted to sign herself Earl Barrenger, oh, what a sweet revenge, and meaningful, too. But that was too close. Earl anything seemed too close to her. She had forgotten that the hero of *The Hot Stars* was named Earl, and that the projected hero of the projected *Loving* was also named Earl.

Concentrating on a name, she thought, All right. What? What? She watched the dairy truck pull into driveway. Charles Dairy. No good. Chuck was nice and masculine though. Dairy? No. No. No. That reminded her of cows. Cows of udders. Udders of...Again no! The truck had trouble manoeuvring into the lane. There. Chuck Lane. Thus, with appropriate labour pains, was Chuck Lane born in a dingy Greenhill kitchen, with the unknowing assistance of the Charles Dairy man.

Chuck Lane.

She was in business.

The portable came out of the pantry. The rickety table danced as she typed the first page and the last page over. Then she did the accompanying letter over. She addressed a new envelope, hurried out to the mail box before she could think of any new reason for changing her mind.

The red maw opened wide, accepted the

big brown envelope, swallowed it whole.

Done. Done. Done.

It was therefore, too late to wonder if Britanica Company, Inc., or Galen Maradick, would remember sending their encouraging mimeographed letter to Mrs Earl Barrenger, and question receiving back synopsis and text from Chuck Lane. A Barrenger, a Lane, who lived at the same address. It was too late, but wonder Kay did. For a moment, doubt shook her as thoroughly as a cat shakes a mouse. But only for a moment. Then she assured herself that Britanica Company, Inc. must send out dozens of mimeograph forms a day, maybe even hundreds. And nobody keeps track of mimeographed forms anyway. It's the replica that count not the forms themselves.

Pleased with her reasoning, she smiled to herself, and went home to type the minutes for the Flower Club.

In her innocence, she waited expectantly. She haunted the door near mail time. It went on for weeks. Mr Fairbanks was beginning to wonder about her, she was sure, before she finally admitted to herself that perhaps she had known all along that these things weren't as easy as she had convinced herself they must be.

A month passed. Spring drained away into summer. Fat and sassy robins quarrelled with overbearing cardinals. The lilacs lost their drooping purple blooms. The weeping willow's mistiness solidified. She hadn't forgotten Britanica Company, Inc., attention: Galen Maradick, but she had decided that it, and he had forgotten her.

At least that was what she told herself as she resolutely fought whole new plots, new characters, new situations. They swam through her mind at the most inopportune moments, often leaving her amber eyes glazed, her lips open to dialogue, when she should have been attending to the proceedings of the Flower Club. League of Women Voters, the Thespians. Having once tasted the joys of creation, she had become addicted to them.

But it was no use to go on. Britanica Company, Inc. had forgotten her, she told herself, as she sighed over the monthly bills.

Then one morning, fat Mr Fairbanks wheezed up to the door. 'Listen,' he complained, 'You don't have no Chuck Lane living here, do you? Something funny about that, isn't there? Who's this Chuck Lane anyhow?'

Mr Fairbanks had very small eyes full of very large suspicions as he peered past Kay's shoulder.

She cried, 'Chuck? Chuck Lane? Why, he's my cousin, Mr Fairbanks. Very very young cousin. On my father's side. Distant, you know. But very very young. He was here for a couple of days. Just passing through. But I'll get it to him. Whatever it is. Yes, don't you worry about it. I'll just send it on to him.' She put out her hand, reaching in an ecstasy of barely concealed hope.

'I didn't think you had no Chuck Lane here,' Mr Fairbanks repeated. But his small eyes, full of large suspicions, continued to search past her shoulders for some sign of the man, of any man, very very young or not, that she might have kept hidden from him all the years he had been on the route, and he held firmly on to the letter.

Kay immediately changed tactics. 'It's an awfully hot day,' she cried. 'Wouldn't you like some iced tea?'

Mr Fairbanks agreed that it was an awfully hot day, agreed that he would certainly like some iced tea. He followed her into the kitchen. He dropped his bag, and sat heavily. He adjusted his weight, and the chair creaked ominously. He put her mail, three advertisements, two bills, she saw at a glance, and *the* letter, on the rickety table.

The long envelope, addressed to Chuck Lane, with Britanica Company, Inc. listed as address to be returned to, seemed to have a glow of its own. It seared her soul from a distance. It tempted and tormented her. She carefully kept her hand away from it while she made tall glasses of tea trimmed with fresh mint, while she discussed the heat, the humidity, the world situation, and at greater length, Mr Fairbanks' onion garden.

He at last heaved himself up to go, neither iced tea, nor heat, delaying him too long from his appointed rounds. He asked, 'You going to get any more mail for that cousin of yours?'

'Oh, no,' Kay told him. I don't see why I should.' At the same time, she started worrying frantically. What now? What do I do now?

'Well, because if you are, you better get that marked care of you or something. I mean, suppose something comes on my day off. There's no Chuck Lane listed here...well, that's different, but if he isn't here, then...'

'He just visited me for a few days.'

'Don't remember you had company. Not for a long time anyhow. Can't think when you last had company, and that's a fact.'

'Oh, it was quite a while ago,' Kay laughed, and then improvised further. 'And over a weekend, too. So...'

Mr Fairbanks looked relieved. Oh, I see. I see. Well, then, that explains it.'

Kay supposed that he didn't want a man in her house, or...

She slid a glance at the envelope on the table. But what was she going to do now? Suppose—?

She couldn't get mail at her house addressed to Chuck Lane. Not anymore. Not with Mr Fairbanks so sensitive to her morals.

'Well, if he does come back, you tell him, will you? You tell him when he uses your address, if he wants his mail delivered, he's just got to use "care of" and your name. I mean, we do the best we can, you know, but we're not mind readers. No, that's one thing we're not.' Plainly savouring the phrase, Mr Fairbanks repeated it. 'Not mind readers, that's one thing we're not you know.'

She walked him to the door, bade him goodbye, smiling a false smile, and damning him heartily in her heart.

She returned to the kitchen at a dead run.

She snatched up the envelope.

From Britanica Company, Inc. Yes.

To Mr Chuck Lane. Yes.

She said a swift prayer, and ripped open the envelope, and sank weakly into a chair, to read...

CHAPTER 3

Door To A Double Life

To read...

Dear Chuck Lane,
We are very enthusiastic indeed about The Hot Stars. *But unfortunately there isn't quite enough text to show to a publisher, especially since you are a new writer, aren't you? Please go ahead and do it as fast as you can. We'll*

push it as soon as we get it, I assure you. The market is good for this kind of thing now. We don't know how long it will last. Let us hear from you soon.

Regards,
Galen Maradick

That was enough.

Kay wasted no time in singing with joy, wasted no time on worry.

She climbed on a chair, and took her copy of what was already written of *The Hot Stars* from the cookie bin. She climbed down, and collected yellow paper, a thick stack of it, and her portable, too, from the pantry.

Paper, portable, pencil, eraser. Coffee, cigarettes.

She settled down to reread what she had already read a hundred times before. *The Hot Stars by Chuck Lane. Chapter 1.* And went on reading the words that marched so sweetly across the yellow page. Finished too soon, she was ready too soon to pick up the story, to send more words marching sweetly across the page. Excited, eager, teeming with ideas, she snapped paper into the portable, raised her hands over the keys. They hung there, fluttering, like small birds over an enemy-occupied nest. The teeming ideas had evaporated into summer heat.

She told herself not to panic. She told herself that she had the rest of *The Hot Stars* written in her head. She told herself...

Two hours later, with the sensation of time oppressing her, worn, wan, and bone-weary, she dug out the shiny yellow-covered paperback that old Mr Avis had recommended so highly.

She slipped it open at random, read...

He enjoyed it most with the girl between his knees, her bottom pushed up high and squirming.

Kay's brows rose. She slapped the yellow-covered book shut. No. That definitely wasn't her style. Now Earl—

Suddenly she found that her fingers were poised over the portable keys. Suddenly, without volition on her part, they came down, hammering out a rapid tattoo, and now words began to march sweetly across the heretofore empty page. She was off, and running, and from somewhere in the distance, she heard faint strains of victory music drifting on the summer wind.

'Now,' Earl said. 'Now and here.'

It was as if they were alone somewhere,

safe and alone in the dark. But they were in Vivian's study, where anyone could walk in on them at any time. Still, though she wanted to, Bonnie couldn't deny him. She was whirlpooled into waves of quick hot hunger, sensually athirst for the hard touch of Earl's body thrusting against hers. She moved with him, savouring her delight, until she could bear it no longer, then she reached for him. Her legs scissored at his hips, and tightened. He began by rocking gently, teasing and tickling, but then hammered and pounded her down and down, until her boneless body melted to him in completion. And just at that moment, Vivian walked in.

By midnight, Kay had written thirty more pages, and carried the adventures of Earl and Bonnie, in *The Hot Stars*, from the first bed to the second to the third.

Kay had also fed Donnie two meals, done the laundry, ironed her best cotton dress.

By dawn, a beautiful summer dawn, the same thirty pages were expanded by five more. Added to the beginning she had already done, they made forty pages. A test which seemed to be something like what Galen Maradick must have had in mind. The forty pages were re-typed and

68

ready for the mail box, for inspection by Britanica Company Inc. But she couldn't send them off until she had rented a post office box so that she could have a safe return address. That solution had come to her, along with the solutions to a number of problems in the text, while she beat on the portable during the night hours.

She would have no more mail addressed to that mythical young cousin of hers, Chuck Lane, come to her house through the hands of curious Mr Fairbanks. Therefore, she had to have a post office box. If Britanica Company, Inc. could do it, then so could Kay Barrenger. But she knew that she couldn't rent a post office box in Greenhill, not with Mr Fairbanks there to see her, not with family, friends, and neighbours, to observe and question her. She decided on a completely new base of operations. She chose Rosemont, a suburb on the other side of the city. It was a status step lower than Greenhill, thus no one she knew would be likely to turn up there.

With that decision made, she called the Rosemont Post Office. She was told that to rent a box from the Federal government one was required to give a home residence and several references, plus certain other information considered pertinent by the Federal government but impertinent by her.

All that, she thought despairingly, would surely defeat the very purpose she had in mind. She was consoled by the conviction that all could be saved by a matter of simple mechanics. For several days, however, she was defeated by the same simple mechanics. At last she managed to figure out how to deal with them, and ignoring a slight suspicion that she might be engaging in a number of criminal acts, she implemented her plan, and sat back to wait the several more days involved.

But waiting was not wasted time. She continued to write on *The Hot Stars*. By the time the mechanics had arranged themselves, she was satisfied with what she had, and that, instead of just forty pages of text, was nearly a completed book. After another early evening to summer dawn session, she wrapped the works, put on her favourite cotton dress, and her make-up, and prepared to start out for Rosemont.

She told herself later that she should have known it was going to be that kind of a day.

Donnie, usually the soul of tact, peered at her from candid blue eyes, blue eyes too peculiarly like Earl's in that moment and demanded, 'What's the matter with you, Mom? Your face looks all lopsided.'

'I'm sleepy, I guess,' she retorted, pouring his milk.

'Why don't you sleep ever.'

'I'm busy. That's why.'

'Banging the typewriter.' Five-year-old scorn had its sting. 'Practising! You!'

It was the story she had told him when he complained that she spent too much time in the kitchen at the broken-down portable. Now she was stuck with it. She wished she had been more inventive at the time the question was originally raised. She sighed. 'Well, I want to be a good typist.'

'What for?'

'It's good to be good at things, isn't it?'

'But you, practising! Come on!'

She ignored that. She got her things together, took up what there was of *The Hot Stars*.

'Is that a present for somebody?' Donnie asked.

She nodded.

'Who?'

Lies. Lies. Lies. Oddly, she was not troubled by them. She decided that she must have a natural instinct for dissembling. 'It's a present for an old school friend,' she told Donnie cheerfully.

'What kind of present?'

'What do you mean, what kind?' That, because she hadn't thought quickly enough. But evasion never worked well on Donnie.

'Just practise papers?' he asked.

His blue eyes were definitely like Earl's. She said, more tartly than she intended. 'Donnie, finish your milk, and then get on the phone and see if Rick is going to the club with his mother. And see if she says it's okay for you to go along.'

'What about you?'

'I have errands.' She patted the brown-wrapped package. 'This. And quite a few others. You'd be bored stiff.'

'No, I wouldn't.'

'Call Ricky,' she said.

He ambled out. Moments later, she heard him yell, 'It's okay, Mom.'

It was six miles, and two bus changes, from Greenhill on the east side of the city, to Rosemont, on the west side of the city.

Kay was somewhere in the middle of the trip when it occurred to her that if she were going to Rosemont because no one she knew ever went there, then she could have just as easily gone by car as by bus. But it was, by then, halfway too late to do anything about that. So she hugged the manuscript to her, and counted the minutes off, and finally alighted in the Rosemont Shopping Centre.

It was an older, more run-down duplicate of the one in Greenhill. Its parking lot was full of Fords and Chevrolets instead of Cadillacs and Mercedes–Benzes. Its hopefully-planted trees had died, and remained where they wilted. Its sidewalks had old and new cracks. Its waste baskets were rusted and overflowing. She picked her way through Wednesday afternoon debris, and found the post office which was hidden behind an overflow of lawn chairs and garden hoses, displayed by the next-door hardware store.

She told the clerk inside that she wanted to rent a post office box. He shoved forms at her through the dusty grill. She took them, went to a stand-up shelf, nervously filled them out. When she returned them, signed Mrs Chuck Lane, for mail addressed to a post office box ought to reach her as either Mr or Mrs, the clerk merely grunted. Her eyes widened in disappointment.

Surely he would ask to see the identification she had so laboriously collected. She had opened a charge account in the name of Mrs Chuck Lane, giving a fictitious address. She had in hand the temporary plate issued her for immediate use. Since she hadn't used it, and didn't plan to, she considered that a very minor infraction of the law, if it was an infraction at all. She had opened a savings account, very small, to be sure, in fact, the minimum acceptable in the name of Mrs Chuck Lane, giving the same fictitious address. She had in hand the bank passbook. Since she didn't plan to use it to defraud anybody, she considered that nobody's business but her own. Thus, well-armed, she waited to be taken over the bureaucratic hurdles.

But no. The clerk gave her another card, a combination, stated his fee and collected it, and turned away.

She thanked his back, retreated to the stand-up shelf. She carefully wrote the return address, Chuck Lane, P.O Box so and so, Rosemont, so and so, on the big envelope. Then she took it to the counter, had it weighed, paid for the necessary postage in a state of shock at what it cost, said a quick silent prayer, and unwillingly relinquished it into the uncaring hands of another clerk.

The long trip home, the two bus changes, the waits in the hot sun, all shifted by, spinning lights fading into darkness.

Kay moved in fantasy, busy with the next book before the first was well on its way.

Miraculously, she didn't really know how miraculously then, *The Hot Stars* sold. She collected her fifteen hundred dollars less Galen Maradick's ten percent. She finished the forty-eight pages necessary to complete the obligatory two hundred in plenty of time, and sent them in, and them promptly turned her attention to remodelling the kitchen.

Amanda and James considered that she had lost her mind, to be spending money she didn't have, and had no prospects of ever getting, for a yellow formica counter, and yellow oven and refrigerator.

Kay didn't argue. She allowed them to harangue her, and completed the kitchen remodelling. Then, in surroundings much more to her liking, she went on to write

Loving. It sold. She wrote *Adventuring.* It sold.

She banked the proceeds, spending it in such small amounts that no one could reasonably question her.

She sat absently through Flower Club meetings, and forgot to take notes, and had to make them up later. The minutes were usually much more interesting than the meetings had actually been. She continued as P.T.A committee chairman. She sewed for the Thespians. She brushed aside Amanda's continuous suggestions that she do something. She worked when Donnie was at school, at play. She worked when Donnie slept.

That spring a year before she had been slightly plump. She grew thinner. Her amber eyes seemed larger, more dreamy. She had learned a lot, and liked it. She was proud of herself. It was easier than it had ever been to remain coolly amused, even under the extreme provocation that was Greenhill.

The Chuck Lane by-line had become a delight.

The first time she had seen it had been quite by accident. Neither Britanica Company, Inc., nor Galen Maradick, nor her publisher, had seen fit to notify her that *The Hot Stars* had come bursting into the light of day. She had waited, counting first weeks, then months. At last beyond patient waiting, she had gone foraging. It was not in Mr Avis' drugstore. It was not in the supermarket newsstand. She began to wonder if *The Hot Stars* was an illusion. A glance fond, possessive, and very reassuring, at her most satisfactory new kitchen, set her fears at rest. Her foraging took her further afield. She spotted *The Hot Stars by Chuck Lane* in an ordinary city drugstore. From a distance, she admired, even gloated over it. She was considering a quick purchase when a deep male voice said, 'Girlie, there you are, all dressed up and no place to go but a soda fountain. Here I am, and likewise. What say we join forces and see what happens?'

She mumbled what she hoped was a polite but firm refusal, and headed for the soda fountain without realizing what she was doing until she found herself closely accompanied by a large male in blue jeans. With a last wild glance at the large male, and an even wilder glance at *The Hot Stars,* she swerved away, and out into sunlight and crowded sidewalk and a return to the familiar confines of Greenhill.

Eventually copies of *The Hot Stars* ended up in her Rosemont post office box. She brought them home, and salted them away in the basement, in a box near Donnie's out-grown clothes, and occasionally went down to cherish them, her first, and at that time, favourite, brainchild. Even more eventually, *The Hot Stars* appeared in Mr Avis' drugstore, and Kay saw him reading it, his plump face etched with lines of sharp agreement, his bald head pink, and all of him oblivious to the line of customers waiting at his cash register.

Soon, *Loving* came out. It became her favourite.

Now there was *Adventuring,* with the cover she considered really quite good, and its prominent place in the supermarket newsstand.

Yes. The Chuck Lane by-line had become a delight, and she couldn't resist slyly enjoying it whenever she had the chance.

But she had no intention at all of disclosing her true identity. There were problems. She knew that very soon she would have to sit herself down and try to figure out how to solve them. Her contracts were getting more and more complicated. They had reached the point where the fine print needed translation by an attorney's trained eye. She didn't know what to do about the bank account. Sometimes she dreamed that she was in prison, convicted of some unspecified crime, and certain that she was guilty. She strongly suspected that she was sinking deeper and deeper into a quagmire, that the door to a double life had been a trap door, in fact, and that she had gone blithely tripping through it, only to be caught there. She strongly suspected that she needed the services, and the advice, of a good lawyer. But, not only did Chuck Lane, the writer, require help, he also required more and more attention.

Meanwhile, Amanda, having trotted around a whole series of her own too-young men, discarded them, for Kay, that is, in favour of pudgy Sam, with whom she held many pleasurable conferences over Kay's shortcomings, her unsociability, her absent-mindedness, and most of all, her lack of enthusiastic response to Sam himself.

Kay absently dated him, agreeing, in cool amusement, with everything he said, until he started talking about paperbacks, about Chuck Lane.

That was when she said, 'Goodbye, Sam.'

She knew it would be weeks, maybe even months before he realized what she meant. She had evaded his ineffectual grab at her waist, twirled away from his downthrust face, closed the door on his sputtering protest.

With Lee Berg gone, she had prepared herself to work...

The evening with Sam, with Sandra and Michael Devlin was a fading memory. She shrugged it away over the portable.

Now there was *Doing It* to consider.

Doing It by Chuck Lane.

Chapter 1.

She read aloud, whispering, *'It was oven-hot. She lay in Earl's arms, her body pressed close to his. The soft slow pace of his breath moved them both. While he slept, she studied the darkness, feeling warm currents gather her in, and grow stronger, until at last, she put her palm against his throat, and slid it downwards along his hard bare chest. It rested there, fingers quivering slightly, and then moved on to savour the flatness of his belly. He murmured and was still again. Instantly her hand ventured on, burrowed cautiously to cup hot velvet. There was a sudden stirring beneath her fingers, and Earl turned to her, wakening suddenly, to throw a hot heavy leg across her hip, to press her back and down, and cover her breasts with quick kisses, and then...'*

Kay paused there, went back to the beginning. *'It was oven-hot...'*

She jumped to her feet. OVEN-HOT. Oven...

She made a dash for the shining yellow refrigerator.

The schedule was clearly written in her own hand. August 25. Four ginger breads for church picnic.

She glared at the calendar. It stood its ground. It didn't change in the face of her red-head's silent but nonetheless broiling temper. It stood its ground all right. August 24.

Then she looked at her watch. She was wrong, all wrong. It was two-thirty a.m and August 25.

She sighed. She gave *Doing It by Chuck Lane, Chapter 1,* a last fond glance. She restacked the yellow sheets, and eased them gently into the treasure chest cookie bin.

She climbed down from the chair,

replaced it at the counter, then put the portable into the pantry next to the jars of apple sauce. She slung pencils, erasers and paperclips into the top drawer of the work cabinet.

Soon the bright, year-old kitchen was full of the spicy odour of gingerbread.

But Kay waiting for the automatic clock to ring, was imagining the scent of Shalimar on satin smooth skin, and naming her next heroine Starrleigh, and her next hero Earl.

CHAPTER 4

Enter The Worried Parents

The scent of Shalimar was gone from the kitchen, but the spicy fragrance of gingerbread lingered.

Kay fixed Donnie's breakfast of cold cereal and milk, and three slices of buttered white toast, and optimistically squeezed orange juice which he disliked, and then peering out at the watery sun, which threatened to disappear entirely behind low-hanging clouds of humidity, she wondered why church picnics always fell on such days, so that the participants sweltered in heat and shivered in damp at the same time.

Donnie cried, 'Listen, isn't it almost time to go?'

'We have two more hours.' She considered unmade beds, tornado struck bathroom. Maybe. Maybe.

'Two more whole hours! We'll miss all the fun.'

'The fun won't start until then.'

'Mo-ther!'

She was hollow-eyed with little sleep. Her fingers itched from the portable now stowed in the pantry next to the jars of apple sauce. She slid a sideways look at Donnie, thinking that suddenly his voice had become Earl's voice. She swallowed spleen, said gently, 'I know you've been waiting all month, but the picnic really doesn't start until eleven, and it's nine now, and...'

'Oh. That's right.' He sat at the table and drank his orange juice without prompting.

She stared at him, amazed. He didn't look a bit like Earl after all. But she immediately began to wonder if, having waited so impatiently for the picnic, he was about to miss it by coming down sick.

He tackled the first of his three slices of toast with good appetite. Mouth full, he said, 'Pretty soon I'm going to be in first grade, hunh?'

'In September. Just three weeks away, Donnie.'

'Kindergarten is for kids, and first grade is for pretty big boys, isn't it?'

Nodding agreement, she waited.

She recognized a ploy when she saw it, but she still didn't know which way Donnie was headed. A moment later, she understood all.

'Pretty big boys have two-wheel bikes, haven't they?'

'Bigger than first grade pretty big boys,' she said.

He gave her what she decided was definitely an Earl look, but was distracted by the sound of a car pulling to a stop outside.

'Now who?' he asked, with pleasure.

'Now who?' she echoed, with no pleasure at all.

She considered a dash for the bathroom. Cold splash on her face. Make-up. Hairbrush. Greenhill standards required that red-headed divorcees appear bustling, bright, and beautiful, no matter what time of the day.

A familiar double knock stopped her.

As Donnie skimmed out to open the door, she relit the flame under the coffee pot.

Her father followed Donnie into the kitchen. 'Kay,' he said smiling, with a fine show of white teeth all his own. 'Kay, dear, how are you?'

'We're going to the picnic,' Donnie told him, giving the big yellow clock a pointed look.

James Mason continued to smile. 'Don't worry. I won't hold you up.'

Kay poured coffee. 'Have some. You can keep Donnie company. He hasn't quite finished breakfast.'

Donnie gave her a mulish look. 'I *have* finished.'

Kay opened her mouth to argue.

James Mason said, 'The fact is, I wanted to talk to you, Kay.'

She closed her mouth.

Small face alight with victory, Donnie said, 'You want me to go, don't you?'

'For a couple of minutes,' James Mason told him.

'You can finish your breakfast later,' Kay told him.

As Donnie loped out, Kay sat opposite her father. 'Something wrong?'

'Wrong, dear? Because I dropped in to see you?' But his smile faded, and faint worry lines appeared in his broad forehead. 'Now why would you think that?'

He was forty-eight years old, a remarkably well-preserved, well-kept, forty-eight. His thick wavy dark brown hair was only slightly touched with silver. His melting dark brown eyes were only lightly etched by debauchery. His chest was broad, his waist flat. He was a dapper dresser, always looking as if he were about to depart for an assignation with an exceptionally inviting woman. Which he sometimes was. His voice was gentle, and slow, his words faintly tinged with England, though the closest he had ever been to London was New York. The touch of broad 'a' came, Kay supposed, from his having seen too many pictures in which the real James Mason was the star. She also supposed she was a bit unfair to her father. But it was extremely difficult to take seriously any man who lusted after the likes of Sweet Cynthia. And lust after Sweet Cynthia,

James Mason certainly did. Every Tuesday and Thursday. At times, Kay suspected, there were others.

Aloud, she said, 'It was just a thought. Somehow, this early on a Thursday morning...' and with a glance at the yellow clock. 'You *did* say that you wanted to talk to me?'

The faint worry lines deepened. The melting dark brown eyes grew solid with concern. 'Kay, dear. I've been thinking about you.'

'About me?' She was sorry she had brought him to the point of the visit. His words made an ominous beginning. 'I'm fine,' she told him, with as much cool amusement as she could muster. 'You shouldn't waste your time thinking about me.'

'Your levity only covers...covers real depression. I know, Kay. I understand,' he said gently.

James Mason, playing the role of the concerned psychiatrist... Really, Kay thought, the cool amusement suddenly real.

He pushed his coffee cup aside.

That meant he was about to get down to business. She waited, relieved.

'Look at you,' he said.

'At me?' Lame, pointless remark. she hastened to add, 'It's pretty early, and I've been busy getting ready for the picnic, so...'

'Picnic!' His gentle smile told her what he thought of church picnics. Told her unnecessarily. She already knew what he thought of them. He wouldn't be caught dead...

'Donnie wanted to go. And I baked four ginger breads,' she said defensively.

'For a woman like you. A woman who is my daughter. Twenty-two years old, and with a young son...'

'Twenty-six years old,' she said firmly.

'Twenty-six?' Her father looked surprised, then rueful. 'Time does fly so.' Then, 'Twenty-six? Really?'

'Really.'

'Look at you,' he went on. 'You're absolutely hollow-eyed. Oh, yes, you are, Kay. And thin as a rail.'

'That's called fashionably slim,' she retorted, knowing the correction would never take with him. He liked buxom women, decidedly buxom women. Now take Sweet Cynthia...

'Hollow-eyed. Thin as a rail. Why,

Margery was just saying to me the other day...'

Margery was Kay's younger sister, a plump twenty-three-year-old matron, with two sons, a thoroughly settled-down husband named Dick Bellows, and more time on her hands than was healthy for her. As they had grown up together, Kay had been the victim of Margery's unquestioning adulation. Since Kay's divorce, she had become the victim of Margery's unquestioning condescension.

Aloud Kay said, 'Margery was always the fat one, and still is so...'

'Kay, dear.' Her father gave her a painful look. 'We all realize how hard it is for a woman to be alone. It's unnatural, unhealthy. You mustn't allow it to make you bitter.'

She slid another look at the yellow clock.

'Now...what I wanted to discuss with you.' He reached into his pocket, drew out his wallet, extracted a cheque. '...is this. You see, I know what a struggle it is. You've been very brave. You've never asked for help. But I worry about you. I want to see you safe, settled in life. I want to see you happy...'

'I'm happy,' she said, but without much hope that she could stop him.

'So I want to give you this small cheque. Donnie will be starting first grade soon. He'll need lots of new clothes, and I can imagine how hard it will be for you. This should...'

'I have plenty of money. Thank you, but I don't need it.'

'...be enough,' James went on blandly. 'And you mustn't think of it as a loan. No. Nothing like that. Just a grandfather buying some small few things for a grandson...'

Wondering just what was loading her father with guilt, Kay raised her voice. 'I don't need it. Truly. Donnie and I make out just fine.'

Which was completely true. There were any number of things she could buy, and wanted to buy, but she hadn't been able to figure out how to do it without accounting for her new hidden source of income. There was, for instance, a new car she had been considering for months. But her family, perhaps everyone in Greenhill knew the exact amount to the penny of the paltry sum Earl sent her to support Donnie. A new car couldn't be passed off as easily as a pair of shoes, even five pairs of shoes.

'You are very brave,' James said, his gentle voice vibrant with emotion, his hands busy returning the cheque to his wallet, the wallet to his pocket.

'Nice of you to think of it though,' she told him.

'Nice! Kay, dear, you don't realize... There's Margery, all settled with a fine husband...' James paused delicately, then, 'Tell me, do you...do you ever hear from Earl?'

'Oh, yes.'

'You do?'

'From his bank anyway. The first of every month. When Donnie's cheque is due.'

'And how is he?'

'Earl? Oh, I wouldn't know.' Or care, she thought fiercely.

'Have you ever thought...?'

'I have not!'

'But if you saw him, Kay.'

'I know everything about Earl Barrenger I want to know. I have seen him maybe three times in the last four years. When he decided to pay Donnie a visit, I might add. Those three times were plenty.'

'Surely, by now. After all, he's an insurance executive, isn't he? Responsible job, that is. And he's older, more sensible, more...?'

'He's twenty-eight years old. He's unmarried. I'm certain that he has been, and still is, totally busy bedding down whatever women he can, putting more notches on his sex belt.'

James winced. 'What a vulgar way to express it, Kay.'

She repressed the urge to tell him that no personal aspersions were intended. She said simply, 'The less we talk about Earl the better.'

James rose. 'No doubt.' He smoothed his dark brown waves. He patted his pocket. 'If you should change your mind...'

'I won't, but thanks again.'

As she walked her father to the door, she decided that it was silly to be thinking about *Doing It.* The typing would have to wait. The morning was practically all gone.

Back in the kitchen again, she found Donnie gulping his breakfast. 'Okay,' he greeted her, burping loudly. 'I'm finished. Can we go now?'

'Don't do that!'

'What?' Aggrieved blue eyes stared at her. 'You said I had to finish, so I...'

'Don't burp. At least don't enjoy it so much.'

'Oh.'

'Yes. Oh.'

'Can we go now?'

Her eyes sought the clock. 'Still an hour, Donnie.'

'Gee whiz.'

'Extraordinary, the language five year olds pick up nowadays, isn't it?' Amanda Mason said from the doorway.

'Six,' Donnie told her, scowling.

Kay stifled a sigh. She had never known how to tell Amanda that Amanda ought to learn to knock at the door, even though it was her elder daughter's door. She had also never known how to tell Amanda that unannounced visits were unwelcome visits even to her older daughter's house.

Amanda stripped off filmy white gloves, set gleaming white purse on the kitchen table, and sat down, pointedly looking at the extra coffee cup that had been James'.

'You just missed him,' Kay told her.

Amanda's blue-green eyes narrowed. 'Who?'

'James.'

'James?'

'Your husband.'

'Oh. Your father.' Amanda didn't bother to conceal her disappointment, her disapproval. 'Your father.'

Donnie, still resigned, mumbled. 'Don't forget the picnic,' and started from the room.

'He,' Amanda said, obviously in deference to Donnie's tender ears, then at the door, 'He,' she repeated, as Donnie threw Kay a single beseeching glance before disappearing into the hallway, '*He* is buying Sweet Cynthia a broadtail jacket.'

So Kay finally knew what James had been feeling guilty about.

Amanda went on icily, 'A broadtail jacket for that...that fat slob!'

Amanda herself could well afford to use such epithets. She was slim-hipped, slender, downright svelte. She wore her forty-four years as well as she wore her simple white lace dress. Her hair was short, a pale silver-blond. Her face was smooth, patrician, and perfectly made up to suggest sophisticated youth.

Kay told her, not believing it herself, 'There's probably a mistake. Want to bet he's just planning a surprise for you?'

94

'I've had the surprise. Haskins called me to double check their measurements. And I am *not* a size forty-four bust!'

'No,' Kay agreed. 'But, really, Amanda, on you a thirty-six bust looks pretty damn good.'

Her mother looked slightly mollified. 'Well, of course. One can overdo these things. Forty-four! I can't imagine what your father is thinking of.' She rose decisively, 'And now...' she stopped. 'But what I wanted to discuss with you...'

'Now?' Kay wailed. 'I have things to do. And Donnie, the picnic...'

Amanda went on, inexorable, as always, '...was what Sandra told me this morning..'

Kay groaned silently.

'The Devlins are delightful hosts. And Sandra does everything so well. So you must have enjoyed your evening with them. But Sandra noticed, now, Kay, sweetheart, please don't fidget like that, she noticed, Sandra, that is that you were rather unpleasant to Sam.'

'Oh, Sam,' Kay said.

'A fine person,' Amanda told her. 'A good upstanding member of the community.'

'A man,' Kay murmured.

'That's right.' Amanda was sharp. 'A man.'

Kay groaned silently.

Amanda, as if she had heard it, said, 'And that won't help, sweetheart. A time will come when it won't be all that easy to find a man.'

'Oh, I don't know. There seems to be something in our family. The women just don't...'

Amanda was complacent. 'True. Still...'

Kay asked brightly, 'Amanda, why are you so sure Sweet Cynthia really is a size forty-four? Maybe Haskins *did* make a mistake.'

Amanda said icily, 'I just happen to be sure.' She glanced at her watch. 'But we mustn't talk about that now, Kay. I have a lot to do. A date at the country club. And then I want to go into town today, too. Haskins is having a sale on some lovely ranch mink!'

Kay's pans of ginger bread disappeared into stacks of angel food, chocolate fudge, and coconut cupcakes.

Donnie disappeared into the quicksand of a potato race.

Kay wished she would disappear, but

96

remained, apparently quite visible. She had hardly taken three deep breaths of thick, murky air, when she was discovered by her sister.

Margery Bellows put a confidential, and confiding, arm around Kay's shoulders, murmured, 'Oh, Kay, I'm so glad you're here! I've been dying to talk to you!'

Kay was immediately transported back in time. She remembered the long before nights when Margery, all adoration, had brought to her for display and sympathy, the secrets, woes and wonders, of troubling teen years. Cautiously, she asked, 'What do you want to talk about?'

'Everything! Life!'

Kay took a second look at her younger sister, wondering where that bright-eyed, self-confident, joyfully expanding matron, had gone to. The shape was the same, all right, but the assured face was suddenly shadowed with drama and discontent.

Margery went on, 'Something's gone wrong, terribly wrong, between Dick and me.'

'Margery!' Kay's concern was feigned. She loved her sister in spite of, or maybe even because of, that annoying adulation which had turned into condescension ever since Kay had divorced Earl and returned to Greenhill.

'I mean it!' Margery's eyes sent quick searching glances past Kay's shoulder, past her own. Then, turning back to Kay, 'Yes, I do.' And her voice dropping into a husky whisper, 'I wait for him, Kay. I lie there, wanting him. Combed, brushed, perfumed. And...and everything. And ready, too. I mean it. Hungry for it. And he...'

Kay hadn't said a word, but Margery stopped. She stopped, holding her breath, insistent that Kay express, shock, horror, sympathy, something.

Kay capitulated. 'My goodness, Margery!' was the best she could bring herself to.

'I don't know what's wrong!' Margery cried, voice rising, then brought sharply down to a whisper again. 'We've only been married three years.'

Kay said, 'A church picnic is hardly the place—'

'I want him so bad. I feel it there. Fire. Burning. Heat. Heat, Kay. You don't know what it's like. You aren't made that way. But oh, for me...'

I don't? Kay asked herself. I'm not? she asked herself.

'Three times a week,' Margery moaned.

'Is that how it's going to be for the rest of my life? Just three times a week?'

'Three times a week?' Kay echoed. 'Oh, I doubt it'll be that for the rest of your life.'

'You don't know. I'm used to it. I want it. Every time I feed the baby...every time I take a bath...I mean, it's like starving, Kay, and there he is...and...'

'And what?'

'He won't. He looks at the baby, and he looks at Jimmie, and he says three chances a week is all he's going to take.'

'The pill?' Kay asked tartly.

'Sure. I take it. What do you think I am?' Margery stopped, gave Kay a quick brown-eyed suspicious look. 'What do you know about the pill? Are *you* taking it?' But she didn't wait for a reply. She couldn't concentrate, for more than an instant, on anything but herself. She went on. 'Dick doesn't believe pills work.'

'Oh, come on,' Kay said.

'Sure, you can laugh,' Margery said bitterly. 'But, Kay, if you only knew...' She choked on her husky whisper. Her round face suddenly dimpled, Her brown eyes shone brightly. Her voice resumed, high and sweet, in trilling welcome, 'Oh,

Ralph! Ralph Parlmeyer, there you are!'

Kay turned slightly, winced when she saw the tall heavy-shouldered man who was the object of Margery's joyful greeting.

She immediately deduced that she was looking at the answer to Margery's three times a week problem with Dick.

Then Margery threw a possessive arm around Kay's shoulder, trilled an introduction.

Kay immediately realized that Margery was simply indulging in her passion for pairing-off. That is, pairing off Kay with whatever man, eligible or otherwise, who came along. Kay winced for herself.

Ralph took her hand, half-bowed over it, smiled. 'Glad to meet you,' he said. It came out, 'Glad ta meetcha.'

He was tall enough to carry those extra-heavy shoulders of his quite gracefully and to wear equally well his tan slacks, darker tan jacket, and open-necked white shirt. His hair was very curly, the colour of wet sand, and cut into an old-fashioned crewcut. He had a large smile, into which, having made his acknowledgement of the introduction, he thrust a large pipe.

'So glad you came,' Margery burbled.

'So am I,' Ralph said. Which came out,

'Som my.' And he widened his wide smile at Kay.

They walked. They sampled chocolate fudge cake, Margery moaning that she mustn't but doing it anyway. They sampled ice cream. They walked. They greeted the church-supporters of Greenhill, for whom the picnic took place on a Thursday, lest Sunday morning hangovers, or golf dates, keep them away.

Then, in an unguarded moment, Kay found herself caught up in one of Margery's adroit manoeuvres. Kay had a firm date for that evening with Ralph Parlmeyer. Sleight of hand accomplished, Margery bustled away.

Ralph removed the large pipe from his mouth, grinned, 'A change of pace will do you good. A few Martinis, some talk...'

Kay, having used up her excuses, was speechless.

'Don't you like Martinis?' Ralph demanded. Which came out, 'Dontch li marteenies?'

Bemused by the peculiarities of his pronunciation, she didn't answer.

'Don't you?' he demanded again. 'I sure do.'

Later that night, the peculiarities of

Ralph's diction were explained. He was an assistant professor of English at a nearby university. And he certainly liked Martinis. In vast quantities.

Kay was at first aghast, and then terrified, by the number of them that he managed to consume. To consume without any noticeable effect beyond a slight brightening of grey eyes, and a tendency to forget to talk like a truck driver from New Jersey.

Besides Martinis, Ralph likes Vogue cigarettes. 'The pipe doesn't go with the drinks,' he told her crisply, leaning forward all wide smile, confidential grey eyes, and strong breath.

But as the embers of a last pink cigarette faded away, he announced that they would have to leave the Greenhill bar where he had gulped, and she had sipped, more Martinis that she was willing, any longer, to try to count.

'We have to go,' he said crisply. 'They don't have Vogue here.'

She agreed happily, thinking ahead to home, Lee Berg, and maybe even the yellow kitchen.

In the car, Ralph made a quick, successful lunge at her, yelped, 'Now

I've got you,' and pasted a wide hot wet mouth on her throat, and a wide hot damp hand on her breast.

With the last breath she was able to take for some few moments, she murmured, 'Time to go, Ralph.' The last breath for some few moments because he had immediately transferred his wide hot mouth to her lips, and fastened it there.

It seemed no more than the necessary good manners to allow him a kiss after all those Martinis.

She allowed it while she wrote the first sentence of *Bored by Chuck Lane, Chapter 1: His arms tightened around her, but his lips touched hers lightly, lightly, in a teasing kiss. 'Oh, Earl,' she whispered...*

She stopped when Ralph's arms wrapped around her, tightly. She stiffened, shifted, smiled, said again, 'Time to go, Ralph.'

'Yes,' he agreed happily. 'It is.' Then, fumbling in his pocket, frowning, 'What did I do with my cigarettes?'

'You smoked them.'

'I'd better stop. Pipe doesn't go with Martinis, you know. You don't mind, do you?'

She did, but said, coolly amused, 'Not at all.'

'You seem in a hurry. I don't want to keep you waiting.'

At first she thought him to be considerably more perceptive than she had imagined. But thinking it over as he pulled up before Mr Avis' drugstore, she decided that wasn't necessarily so. In the era before the pill, a drugstore stop, after all those Martinis, probably wouldn't have been for cigarettes. And what had that remark about not wanting to keep her waiting actually meant?

She went in with him. He seemed neither concerned, nor embarrassed. He bought his two packs of Vogue while she stopped to look at the paperbacks.

Adventuring by Chuck Lane.

She smiled at the tall, dark-haired, bare-chested man who stood over the small blond girl.

Her evening was saved.

'Do you read them?' Ralph asked.

'Sometimes,' she admitted.

'Don't look so guilty. Everybody does.' He took her arm, slightly damp fingers stroking the inside of her elbow. 'If a writer wants to be read, he has to get paperback distribution. Either first or last. Wide audience, you know. Widest. And what a business.' He helped her into his car, closed the door, leaned there, grinning enthusiastically. 'Wide open, too!'

'Wide open?'

'Anybody can write them. It's a trick,' he explained. With that, he walked around the car.

She had not imagined that Ralph could say anything to interest her so much. The moment he got in beside her, she asked, 'What kind of trick? What do you mean?' If there was something she didn't know yet, some easy way to do it, then she meant to find out about it.

'Formula,' he explained, getting the car into motion. 'That's all it is. You can write one in ten days.'

'I could?'

'Well, maybe not you. But I could. And the money in it!'

'Have you?'

'Oh, I don't have time.' He nodded. 'But...but all you do..you just sit down, get started. With sex, of course. And get some sex into every chapter. And that's it.'

She noticed that his words picked up speed as he spoke. She noticed that he doubled one large hand into a fist and crammed it into his lap. She also noticed, at last, with a good deal of relief, that she was home.

The relief was premature.

Ralph was as adroit in getting rid of Lee Berg as Margery had been in saddling Kay with him for the evening.

Kay found herself alone in the centre of the living room with Ralph advancing upon her, beaming, 'You're a wonderful conversationalist, Kay,' but clearly not having conversation in mind.

She made a tactical retreat towards the hallway, but found herself swung daintily to the sofa.

'And that,' Ralph laughed, 'is only one advantage of putting a big man and a small girl together.'

She decided not to ask him what the other advantages were.

'And now, about sex,' he said, as he plumped down beside her, and wrapped her in long firm arms. 'About sex, Kay...'

'What?'

'The ordinary way...that's just absolutely nothing anymore. Everybody knows about that.'

'What?' she repeated, not sure she heard him right, and hoping she hadn't.

'So you have to ring in what's new,

different, exciting.'

She realized then, that he was *talking* about sex in paperback books. But what he was *acting* out was not actually new, nor different, nor to her, particularly exciting.

She murmured, 'You know so much about it, Ralph. You ought to write a book. Really, Ralph.'

'I could,' he said. 'I could all right. If I had the time.'

She said brightly, 'And speaking of time. It *is* rather late. Such a nice evening. But now...'

His arms enfolded her. He whispered intensely, 'But you want to, Kay. You know you want to. Or are you the kind that has to be persuaded?'

She plucked ineffectually at the big hand that clasped her breast, the other big hand that clutched her thigh.

She sighed. 'Now Ralph...' and found herself flat on her back with one of Ralphs' big hands at the neck of her dress, and the other at his belt. She thought of the drugstore stop, and knew she had been half right. That kiss in the car had presaged more to come. A part of her mind murmured, Excuse the expression, please. At least it had to Ralph. In the pre-pill era that drugstore stop would certainly have meant exactly what it reminded her of.

'Ralph,' she said firmly, though slightly choked, 'you're a nice guy, and I like you a lot, but I think you've got the wrong idea.'

He gave no sign of having heard her. He lowered his bulk towards her, belt opening, mouth opening, eyes closing.

'Ralph,' she said gently. 'Ralph? Don't be ridiculous.'

He still gave no sign of having heard her.

She aimed a small knee at his groin, a small fist at his face. 'I don't like to be persuaded,' she explained as he drew himself up. 'Thank you for all those delicious Martinis,' she said, as he prepared to leave. 'Good night,' she said, as he closed the door behind him.

And from the bedroom down the hall, Donnie cried, 'Mama, is that you?'

He rarely called her that any more, having graduated to Mom at about the same time that he graduated from kindergarten,

She dashed into his room.

'Mama?'

'Just me,' she crooned, sitting beside

108

him. 'What's wrong?'

'I had a bad dream.'

'What about?'

'I guess I don't remember.'

'Then forget it.'

'Cocoa would help,' he said wistfully.

She thought it might help her, too. 'Okay. Cocoa then.'

She made it quickly, brought the cups in.

He was waiting, bright-eyed, conversational. While he sipped, he asked, 'Why is Grandpa worried about you?'

'You were listening, Donnie! That's not right.'

'I just heard him, that's all.'

'He's not really worried. That's just a figure of speech.'

'But he said...'

'Donnie! You're finished, and I'm finished, and you're stalling.'

He slid down to his pillow. 'I can't imagine why he would say that, not if he didn't mean it.'

She didn't answer Donnie. She took the cups back to the kitchen, and looked at the yellow clock.

It was not quite midnight.

She had expected it to be later. Those

109

hours with Ralph had seemed absolutely interminable.

She grinned to herself. If James had seen her in Ralph's arms, James would have been even more worried. Because there had been nothing there. Nothing at all.

She got out portable and paper. She took the thick manuscript from the cookie bin, and kicked off her shoes, and lined up pencil and carbon and cigarettes, and, whistling softly to herself, she went to work on *Doing It*.

CHAPTER 5

The CSTB

With that petulant assurance which is the mark of the new breed of women, June said, 'Every girl has the right, yes, that's just what I mean the RIGHT, to enjoy sex. Not just sometimes. Not just accidentally. But always. And deliberately. And if her husband can't or won't, provide her with the means to achieve that right, then she is morally entitled to find fulfilment elsewhere.'

'I'm all for that,' Earl told her, smiling, and then burying his smile against her breasts, his breath touching one rose-petal nipple, while he wished that she would concentrate on him, on him, and on the bed where they lay, on the purpose for which they lay on the bed, instead of providing him with the apologia she insisted on providing, one he had already heard umpteen times from the other married women with whom he had lain on other beds.

'My husband,' June went on, 'treats me like a convenience. A blender, say. You use it when you need it, and then you think it's just great. But the rest of the time, and that's most of the time, you just keep it standing on the counter, polished and ready to go, and very much admired by you and all, but absolutely useless. I have feelings, too,' she concluded, and put her tongue in Earl's ear.

The sweet words, having marched sweetly across the page, stopped abruptly.

Kay's small hands hung over the portable, fluttering like suddenly uneasy birds. She had an odd feeling. She wondered if she were becoming psychic. Weeks before she had done the scene to which, Margery, setting up her justifications at the church picnic that morning, had definitely been heading.

Kay brushed red-gold hands from a damp forehead. She dropped her hands to her lap. She left June and Earl in bed together, and started thinking about Margery and Dick. The final typing of *Doing It* came to a full stop.

It came to a full stop for a long time. For, as she considered Margery and Dick, and their two very small sons, and contemplated what could happen, and tried to think what to do about the four of them, there was a knock at the door.

Kay sighed. She didn't think she was up to company. She was so busy thinking of that that she forgot the manuscript spread out on the table, the portable. She forgot Chuck Lane.

She shoved her chair back, swearing softly, and trotted out to see who was bothering her at an ungodly hour, after an ungodly number of Martinis. Memory of the martinis brought back memory, definitely unwelcome, of Ralph Parlmeyer. She shuddered over instant visions of the big man returned to bay his desire at the non-existent moon, and bringing down the laughter of Greenhill on her sorely-tried head.

She leaned against the door, whispered a cautious, 'Who's there?'

'What's the matter with you, Kay?'

She very nearly giggled in her relief. She pulled the door open.

Her brother-in-law, Dick Bellows, gave her an aggrieved look, and plunged past her.

'Who's there?' he mocked her. Then, 'Who did you expect? Anybody I know? Sorry to disappoint you. But it's only me. The Big Bad Wolf of Greenhill.'

She was dizzied by fumes of bourbon. She closed the door gently, clung to it. 'What's the matter with *you*, Dick?'

'I saw your light. I was driving by. I can't stay home anymore so I was driving by. And I saw your light. So I...'

'You thought that maybe a cup of coffee...'

'Yes. Please. Driving by...' He staggered to the kitchen, and she followed.

She relit the flame under the percolator, while he plunked himself down at the table.

The completed pages, pristine white around beautiful black print were spread out under his elbows.

He was medium-sized and proportioned,

but robust in that particularly compact way that suggested football fields and baseball diamonds and hockey courts. In fact, Dick loathed all physical activity, and the contact sports most of all. He had very good, clean-cut features, and Kay had often wondered if it was in protection of those good, clean-cut features that he avoided even an innocuous game of balloon catch with his two small sons. He was twenty-four now, a year older than Margery, and when they had married four years before, Greenhill had grinned knowingly over its cocktail glasses and suggested that the Masons and the Bellows had brought up two exceptionally moral kids.

Kay suspected differently, but considered it none of hers, or Greenhill's business. But she thought, as Chuck Lane suddenly intruded, and she saw the pristine sheets of *Doing It* slowly crumpled under Dick's sweatered elbows, that he, and Margery, were apparently determined to make it her business, if not Greenhill's.

She whisked the sheets away, slid them cautiously to the other side of the table. She reached unobtrusively for the portable.

Dick demanded, 'Do you have to fuss?

I don't drop in at midnight every night in the week.'

'Thank goodness.'

'...so you know there's a reason, don't you? You must know there's a reason.'

'You wanted a cup of black coffee.'

'Funny girl!' Dick looked at her sorrowfully. 'Can't you be serious?'

'I can try,' she offered, unwillingly.

'Then do,' he demanded.

'Shall I pour the coffee before it perks away?'

'Please.' His too-bright eyes narrowed with self-pity. 'Yes, Kay. Coffee, and then...'

'A listening ear?' She filled a cup for him, one for her. She cast a careful look at the portable.

Dick caught the glance, said, 'Writing letters, hunh? Well, they can wait, can't they? Kay, listen, what the hell's happening to Margery anyway?'

'How do you mean, Dick?'

'You're older,' he said. Apparently he thought she might not like the sound of that. He amended it quickly. 'I mean, after all, you've been divorced, you've been around. You know how things are. So...'

'What's that got to do with what's gotten into Margery?'

He took a sip of coffee, made a face, shoved the cup aside. 'Kay, listen, you got anything to drink besides this stuff?'

'Orange juice?'

He shuddered.

'Tomato juice?'

He groaned.

'I don't have anything that you want.'

'I was afraid of that.'

'Besides, you've had enough.'

'Not nearly enough. I hate to go home. That's what it is. I have to get good and drunk before I go home.'

She didn't intend to ask him why, and didn't ask him why.

That didn't concern him; he wasn't listening for questions. He went on, 'And it's all because of Margery. She's at me all the time. You know what I mean? I hardly get set to go to sleep, and she's there, pulling at me. For Pete's sake, Kay, a man's got to get some rest, doesn't he?'

Kay waited.

'Sex in the morning, sex at night. It's a good thing I don't get home for lunch. That girl...she's...she's...'

'Insatiable?'

116

Dick looked relieved. 'Then you see it, too, hunh? You can tell?'

'No. I'm just picking words out for you.'

'I'm as good as the next man,' he said. And added, 'At least I think so, thought so. But these...these...well, for Pete's sake, these demands, Kay. She's already got the two boys. What else does she want?'

'Aren't you mixing your subjects?'

'I do not intend to copy some people and have eleven children,' Dick said, bourbon dignity written plainly on his face.

'You needn't.'

'That's what she says!'

Kay sighed. 'Well, I don't know what to say.'

'You don't have to say anything.' His too-bright eyes narrowed again. 'Maybe it's something that runs in the family.'

Kay grinned. 'Maybe. But what is the *it* that you have in mind?'

Dick lurched to his feet. 'All I can say is, she better quit demanding so much. There's plenty of women around.'

Kay grinned again. 'With *their* demands? You can end up a pretty busy boy.'

Dick ignored that, followed his own train of thought. 'I tell you, they come in to look at cars, that's what they say, but if I even tipped them half a wink, well, then...'

Kay forebore to ask why, if he felt his wife was making excessive wifely demands, he should be threatening to seek out a source of additional demands. Instead, seeing the opportunity he had offered, she seized it. She said, 'I've been intending to talk to you about just that, Dick.'

He looked at her blankly.

She rushed on. 'I want to buy a new car. What do you recommend?'

His favourite subject broached, he was instantly diverted. He sat down again. He braced his elbows on the table and launched into a warm, intense, in-depth discussion of what his agency had to offer.

It was the next evening.

Sam had called three times to remind Kay about the first P.T.A meeting of the coming school year. Each of the three times he had offered to pick her up. She had declined with thanks, saying it was just a nice walk away. Her former associates in the kindergarten division, graduating, as she was, along with offspring into first grade, had called her, too, and offered to pick her up.

Having maintained her independence in the face of Greenhill's urgency, and bewilderment, nobody walked even a block, ever, if it could be avoided, she could think of absolutely no excuse for forgetting the meeting. Short of amnesia, or total collapse.

Thus, combed, curried, sleeked into a tan linen suit, a glow of white organdy under her chin, she set out in soft blue twilight for the Greenhill Elementary School.

Her mind was on the Rosemont Post Office, where, she imagined, there was a vitally important letter awaiting Chuck Lane. Her heart was on that stack of still-untyped pages that awaited her in the cookie bin.

As she settled herself in the school conference room, avoiding Sam's triumphant wave, she thought grimly that she ought to have developed amnesia, or had a total collapse. It had suddenly occurred to her that she would have to go through twelve years of P.T.A. She shuddered. But moments later, the hum of voices had faded. She wrote dialogue in her mind.

119

But then sweet escape became capture. Voices. A rude elbow in her ribs. A raucous whisper.

'Take it. You've just been elected secretary.'

The *it* was a large heavy notebook.

The raucous voice belonged to Mrs Planter, a thin, sharp-faced woman, nervous mother of twins. Kay knew her from their shared year of service in the kindergarten.

Kay accepted the large heavy notebook, falsely smiled her delight, and promptly returned to Starrleigh and Earl, manoeuvring now in *Bored*. They were in a corn field. Shadows...No. Sunset...Sunrise.

She laughed softly, and drew her mouth from his. Her movement put her lips against his shoulder, and then her teeth dug in and held and stung, arrowing sudden pain through him, and, in the strange alchemy of love, pain became desire. He drew her to him. His fingers stroked her face, and then cupped her cheeks in big hot hands that forced her head back. He kissed her hard and deep, his tongue moving in the mirror of that intimacy for which they both hungered. She clung to him when he moved over her, clung tight and hard, and their naked straining bodies locked in heaving struggle for a long time before they were still in the pale light of the pink dawn.

Some time later the raucous and rude voice and the spearlike elbow of Mrs Planter intruded again. 'He is (nudge) absolutely right!'

Kay sighed, and tuned in to Sam Golden's anguished voice, raised to be heard over ripples of virtuous agreement '...and so I say to you, it is your responsibility, your duty, your privilege, to save our children from this.. this filth.' He paused to allow applause.

Kay raised her eyes to look at him.

He held aloft, for all to see, a paperback book. Tall, dark-haired man, small kneeling blond girl.

Kay squinted with professional curiosity. A very good cover. She sat back with professional satisfaction. Chuck Lanes' *Adventuring.* She straightened with personal outrage. What did Sam Golden think he was doing to her?

Meanwhile, Greenhill matrons, politely in some cases, enthusiastically in others, supplied the applause for which he had paused. Then he went on, 'I propose, therefore, that this P.T.A, here, in its all-grade meeting, set up a committee to investigate such books, to find ways and means of preventing their distribution, to call attention to their dangers to our own dear community, our county, our state, and our nation.' Another pause. More applause. 'Thank you. And I further propose that our distinguished co-worker, Kay Barrenger, who has already proven herself as a leader, be its chairwoman, and lead us in this good fight.'

Kay murmured. 'Move. You fool. Haven't you ever read Robert's Rules of Order?'

'That's just wonderful,' Mrs Planter cried. 'It's the thing that will put Greenhill on the map.' She bounded to her feet, all angles and flashing eyes, her print dress snapping like a banner in a breeze. 'And what we ought to do, we ought to look into the library, too, while we're looking. They've got books by that Virginia Woolf. Oh, yes, they have. I've seen them. Everyone knows from the movie what kind of rough life she leads. And the way she talks, her and her husband, you can imagine her books all right.'

Sam smiled weakly. 'One danger at a time, Mrs Planter, but thanks. Now these paperback books...'

The meeting collapsed into a cross-fire of cross-aisle conversations.

Sam appealed for order. It was restored only when that subject, and certain peripheral problems, such as sex in the high school, had been thoroughly discussed. With order restored, Sam requested a second for his proposal.

'The motion,' Kay murmured in small defiance, and then, in large defiance, rose to say, 'Mr Golden, I just want to refuse to be on the committee, so take my name from the motion. If you want to have the committee, that's your business and the P.T.A's. But I don't believe in censorship. And,' she finished lamely, 'I don't have time.'

'We'll give you plenty of help,' Sam said gently.

'It's a good cause,' Mrs Planter cried. 'What's more important than our kids.'

'The motion,' the chairwoman yelled.

'Just a minute,' Kay said.

Amid general uproar, there was a vote.

Kay grimly recorded the result in her notebook. Mrs Kay Barrenger was elected chairwoman of the Committee to See about Those Books, the CSTB, as she abbreviated it in the minutes of P.T.A.

Later, when she was leaving, Sam bustled after her. 'I'll drive you home, Kay.'

'I think I'll walk,' she told him.

'Walk? Alone? After dark? Why, Kay, my dear...'

'Sam,' she asked seriously, 'what could possibly happen to me in Greenhill?'

'All sorts of things,' he said darkly.

It seemed hardly worth the argument. So Kay allowed Sam to drive her home, to lead her to her door, to linger while she paid off Lee Berg, and watched him lope away.

Then Sam proceeded to try to show Kay just what could happen to her in Greenhill. He was all hot breath and searching lips, all hands and hugs.

She thought sadly that it was a shame. There was nothing there. Nothing there at all. All hands, hugs, and searching lips not withstanding.

She remained coolly amused, but firm.

Aggrieved, he decided that he wanted to talk about *those* books.

She sent him tactfully on his way, and went to work on *Doing It*.

She liked to tease him. She liked seeing his face go taut and dark with desire, and hear his breath quickened, and know that pretty soon he wouldn't listen to her, no matter what she said. So when his hands slid down her thighs to the edge of her skirt, and pulled at it, she caught him by the wrists, 'And no, no,' she said, at the same time clenching her thighs together hard because she knew she was weakening, and in a minute, she wouldn't be able to say, 'And no, no,' again. But that time he fooled her. He went still, his hands resting against her knees, waiting. She waited, too, for as long as she could, which was the space of a single breath. Then she cried, 'Earl...' And pulled her skirt up and drew his hands to her bared thighs...

CHAPTER 6

Trapped

She had arranged to meet Dick at the agency at eleven. Although she had fought the portable until three, and spent the rest of the night in unpleasant reliving of the P.T.A meeting, she was up early. By nine, the laundry was in the washer, Donnie was fed, talked to, and off on a city trip with Rick and Rick's mother. The kitchen was cleaned up, the living room dusted, and

Kay was dressed and ready to go.

She, therefore, had the luxury of two free hours. She considered *Doing It,* innocently reposing in the cookie bin. But her eyes burned and her fingertips ached. She decided to leave *Doing It* where it was, and awarded herself two hours off.

But she didn't know what to do with two hours off. She had managed to write four novels in eighteen months. Four. How many hours of work? How many reams of yellow paper, of white? How many fantasies?

Her restless feet took her wandering. Aimless steps led her to the basement. There, among Donnie's outgrown clothes, and toys, and baby furniture, saved, but never to be used again, she thought sadly, she had hidden copies of the final draughts of her books, and author's copies of *The Hot Stars, Loving,* and *Adventuring.*

She gloated over them, forgetting to be sad. It was a pleasure she rarely afforded herself, and she enjoyed it so much, enjoyed being Chuck Lane so much, that time sped by, and she was twenty minutes late for her appointment with Dick.

He told her that she had a smudge on her chin.

She rubbed it away vigorously answering, 'I'll have to clean up the basement one of these days.'

He ignored that seeming irrelevancy. 'I thought you weren't going to show up.'

'Oh? Why?'

'I mentioned about your new car to Margery, and she just laughed. She said you couldn't possibly buy a new car.'

'Oh? Why?' Kay repeated, coolly amused.

'Money,' Dick said.

'I'll manage.' Her tone was dry. Her amber eyes had begun to sparkle, lit by small flames of anger. It seemed that, as always, she was the main topic of conversation to occupy her family. She wondered, all things considered, how they found the time.

Dick went on, 'And that's what your father said, too.'

'Not to mention Amanda,' Kay's tone was still dry.

'They worry about you, you know.'

'No need.' To change the subject, she said, 'How's your head today? Still suffering ill effects?'

Dick, aggrieved that she had been so tactless as to mention their last meeting, embarrassed that both he, and she, remembered it, muttered, 'I guess I talked too much that night.'

'A little,' she agreed, tranquillity restored. 'Now about my car...'

He, reversing the usual routine, probably at the careful instruction of Margery and Amanda, first led her to look at the cheapest, smallest, least interesting new car he had to offer.

Kay handled him, and his intentions, adroitly. With manufactured objections concerning road safety and upkeep, she manoeuvred him three steps up in price range. With wistful wandering, she manoeuvred him the rest of the way to the car she had picked out the moment she stepped into the showroom. It was a long emerald-green hard-topped convertible. Sleek, dashing, sophisticated. A Chuck Lane car. A car for her.

Dick, torn between agency loyalty and family loyalty, made a few half-hearted objections.

She blithely ignored them.

He might have had more to say, but the sales manager wandered over. His eyes made a careful inventory of Kay, from red-gold bangs, to yellow silk suit, to yellow peau de soie shoes. He seemed to think it was her kind of car, too. He whipped out a sales contract, a ballpoint pen, and a huge grin. Dick went happily to work. He wrote, calculated, wrote, said finally, 'Now let's see, Kay. Terms. You'll want the longest possible period of instalment payments. That'll add...'

'I'm paying cash,' she said.

He whistled, then frowned, then demanded, 'Listen do you know what this car costs?'

'It's cheaper to pay cash,' she said.

The sales manager wandered back. 'Everything all right here, Mrs Barrenger?'

'Oh, yes,' she dimpled. 'I'm paying cash, of course. I'll bring the cheque in the end of the week. Will you have the car ready for me by then?'

'You bet. You can have it this afternoon, if you want to. About four?'

'Let's settle for tomorrow.' Without pause, Kay snatched the pen from Dick's limp fingers, signed her name to the contract, gave the emerald-green convertible a loving glance, and drifted out on a joyful pink cloud. Done. Signed for. Almost delivered...

The pink cloud dissolved under her when she arrived home. She bounced on the rocks of reality with a hard bruising thump.

The news had travelled fast.

Amanda was waiting.

Amanda was not only waiting, but she was waiting in the kitchen. She was not only waiting in the kitchen, but she was foraging.

As Kay came in, warned by Amanda's baby-blue convertible parked outside, Amanda's outstretched hand was drawing the treasure chest cookie bin along the top of the yellow refrigerator. Her blue-green eyes were narrowed with effort. Her silken white fingers strained. Her pink lips shaped to a curse.

Kay gasped, cried out, 'Oh, damn and blast,' and in a belated, but related action, wildly turned her ankle, and staggered, and collapsed into a chair.

Amanda's silver-blond head turned, but her outstretched hand remained on the cookie bin. 'What's the matter, sweetheart?'

'I'm afraid I turned my ankle.' Leaning over, Kay vigorously massaged her calf.

'I'm starved,' Amanda said. 'Soak it in hot water. Or is it cold?'

Kay leaped to her feet. 'The cookie bin's empty. I've been too busy to bake. I'll get you something from the pantry.'

Amanda gave her a narrow look. 'Your ankle?'

'Oh, it's nothing.' Kay escaped into the pantry, rummaged longer than she had to, seeking equilibrium she had lost, and returned, imagining that she was carrying raisin bread, but bringing with her instead, the rickety portable. 'Just what you love,' she said triumphantly.

Amanda gave the portable a narrow look. 'Your nerves, sweetheart...really. Old maid jitters, I suppose.'

Kay gulped, retreated once again to the pantry, found the raisin bread, and went bustling about the kitchen. Busy toasting, buttering, pouring coffee, she chattered, delaying the moment of truth. She told Amanda about the CSTB. Amanda was not amused. She told Amanda about Ralph Parlmeyer. Amanda was not sympathetic. She told Amanda about Donnie's visit to the city with Rick and Rick's mother. Amanda was not interested. But Amanda *was* patient.

She waited until Kay had run down, and sat down. She waited until Kay said brightly, 'I bought myself a car today.'

'I know. That's why I'm here.'

Kay nodded, attempting to cling to brightness, to feel tranquillity, to summon cool amusement.

Amanda thoughtfully lit a cigarette, thoughtfully blew out smoke, thoughtfully pursed pink lips, and said, 'I suppose that's a natural thing.'

'Natural?'

'For women who live alone, who have empty lives, and, of course, any woman alone must have an empty life, I suppose it is quite natural to suffer from nerves,' she raised her voice, raised it as if Kay had spoken, but in fact Kay had remained quite silent. Amanda raised her voice argumentatively, '...natural for eccentricity to set in.'

Relieved, therefore incautious, Kay snapped up the bait. 'Eccentric, Amanda?'

Amanda raised her delicately-tilted nose, smoothed her silver-blond waves. 'I consider it quite eccentric for a woman who has absolutely no money, practically no support from her former husband, no job, no anything, and nothing in sight because of her own peculiarities, for such a woman to sign a contract to buy for cash a car she knows absolutely that she can't possibly pay for, that's eccentric. It's probably also criminal in some way.'

'I can pay for it,' Kay said, achieving tranquillity.

Amanda went on, Kay's retort, unheard or unaccepted. 'And that is particularly true when such a woman has already contracted for the remodelling of a kitchen, on which she must still be paying instalments plus interest. And...'

Kay cut in, 'Amanda, I have a confession to make.'

Amanda stopped so suddenly that Kay didn't have time to figure out what her confession was going to be.

However, she drew a long, slow breath, and plunged. 'The kitchen is already paid for. And the car...well, I'll be able to pay for it because...because...' having plunged, she had to swim. She did. 'You see, I know it's terribly silly of me, but as you say a woman alone...I'm a contest enterer, Amanda.' As Kay uttered a quick silent prayer of thanks to the gods that provide liars with lies, she went on, improvising. 'You know...all those contents in the women's magazines. Slogans. Write fifteen words about why you use, or like, or...'

Amanda's thoughtful face relaxed into sympathy. 'Why, Kay, really, sweetheart...'

'I know.'

'What a ridiculous way to waste your time.'

'The kitchen. Now the car...'

'Still utterly ridiculous.' Amanda drew on black gloves. 'But James will be relieved. He thought...'

'I suppose you all thought I'd lost my mind.' Kay, having rescued herself, became a might malicious. 'Eccentric. Wasn't that the word?'

'Never mind, sweetheart. Now that we know your little secret...' Then, 'By the way, why didn't you tell us?'

'So ridiculous,' Kay murmured.

'Of course, sweetheart. And eccentric. I'm glad you see it. And I won't say a word.' Amanda rose, headed for the door. 'I must be on my way. I nearly forgot my fitting at Haskins'. Your father is buying me a mink jacket, you know. Ranch. Lovely. Much nicer than broadtail, of course. And, Kay, you ought to change your attitude a bit.'

'My attitude?'

'About Ralph Parlmeyer. A charming man. Margery says so. And very much your type. Literate, and all that. You'd fit nicely into the groves of academe.'

'He smokes pastel cigarettes.'

Amanda looked pained, but recovered quickly. 'Sweetheart, every man has his little peculiarities. If you knew about your father...'

Kay thought of Sweet Cynthia's Tuesdays and Thursdays, and nodded unverbal agreement.

'Oh, dear,' Amanda cried, 'I'm late for the country club, too.'

Kay thought of young Carl Hessler, and once again nodded unverbal agreement.

Amanda swept out with a parting shot. 'Lovely dress, Kay. You must spend too much time on these contests.'

To her mother's back, Kay murmured the rehearsed but unnecessary lie, 'From college days. The style just came back.'

Morning of the big day. The emerald-green hard-top convertible day. The Rosemont branch of the State National Bank was busy.

Kay waited to fill out her withdrawal slip, waited before the teller's window, waited while the teller finished an enthusiastic conversation with another teller. Watching the two, one male, young, and tentative, the other female young and aggressive, she was reminded of two birds involved in a love minuet on the wing.

The young teller, female, young, and aggressive, finally turned to her and smiled. 'Hi, Mrs Lane.'

Kay shuddered. She passed over the withdrawal slip. It was, she thought, a symbol of the suburbs that anonymity was impossible.

Mrs Chuck Lane.

It had a sinister sound.

She would never accustom herself to responding casually to it. The *Mrs* distressed her. But, she told herself, she could hardly expect to be called Mr Chuck Lane, could she?

The teller dimpled. 'Certainly is a large withdrawal.'

'New car,' Kay told her, and stuffed the wad of bills into her purse. Not only was anonymity impossible, but also private business.

She would have preferred a cheque, but the thought of depositing a cheque made out to Mrs Chuck Lane, in her bank account, or even a cheque made out to Kay Barrenger, but signed by Mrs Chuck Lane, made her decidedly nervous. Even more nervous than transporting that thick wad of cash from the Rosemont bank to her bank in Greenhill.

Outside, she cast a longing glance at the Rosemont Post Office, tempted to wend her way between fading beach chairs, and tilting umbrellas, to check her box. Perhaps Britanica Company, Inc.? But she still had to stop in her Greenhill bank, and she knew Donnie would be home any minute. She fought the temptation and won, telling herself that such victories were good for the soul. And to underscore the victory, she told herself that she wouldn't return to Rosemont until *Doing It* was finished.

The large deposit at the Greenhill bank occasioned the raising of two finely-tweezed and pencil-darkened eyebrows, but no other comment. She considered the practical chores done, but one.

She went to the agency. She admired her beautiful new car, and paid for it, and with a joyful smile at Dick's relieved face, she departed.

She arrived home only moments before Donnie. From then on, until eight o'clock, there were more practical chores.

But by eight, Donnie was fed, entertained, bedded, watered, prayed with, and the light was out.

By eight-ten, Kay was in her pyjamas, and hunched over the typewriter, banging out a parade of words that marched sweetly across the white page.

She unbuttoned his blue shirt slowly, put her head against his bared chest, butting and burrowing, as if seeking access to his pounding heart. 'I want you,' she whispered. 'I want you, want you.' The cool autumn air turned hot around them, enclosing them, as he pulled at her sweater and then her bra and finally reached the silken heat of her rounded breasts. He couldn't speak and didn't have to, for then her satiny curved hips were below his, pressing, and her legs were clasped around him, clasping him to her and quivering spasmodically. Their quarrel had been too deep, the separation too long. This was their first time together since, and he couldn't control himself. It was too hard and fast, and he knew, with a part of his mind, that he hurt her. He hurt her, and himself, too, with the urgency that was beyond any restraint. Later, when she trembled in his arms, he hated himself. But later still, when they moved together again, and it was slow and sweet and long-lasting, her eyes widened, and he felt the deep internal quivering, he knew it was right for them both.

Kay worked on and on. By three-thirty a.m an awed and jubilant labourer found herself typing THE END to the strains of distant valedictory music.

The emerald-green car seemed to know the way to Rosemont.

Kay, in the first flush of ownership, and the second flush of accomplishment, sang aloud joyfully, and periodically touched the new-wrapped, and addressed, final draft of *Doing It.*

She thought, as she parked, of that first long, and unnecessary bus trip to Rosemont. She had lost count of how many times she had been there in the past eighteen months. At first, almost every day that she could manage, hopefully dialling the combination to peer into shadowy emptiness. Then twice a week. Finally, more blase with success and time, she made the trip every two weeks. That was less risky, more convenient, and definitely not satisfying.

She had noted the change in Galen Maradick's letters. That increase in warmth which was a measure of her success. She had been startled by the first fan letter she received, embarrassed by the second, frightened by the third. From the third on, she viewed with caution anything forwarded on to her by Galen Maradick. But, whatever it was she read it for hints, then destroyed it before returning home. Torn into bits and flushed away in a department store ladies' room, it had no reality. No more reality than the debris which she just as carefully tore into bits and flushed away after every night's work.

The car was given attentions such as her old one had never received. She closed the windows, locked the doors. Satisfied that security standards had been maintained, with *Doing It* clutched in both anxious hands, she started for the Rosemont Post Office.

A familiar voice, quick startled words, snared her.

'Why, Kay, what are you doing in Rosemont?' Sandra Devlin, lovely, willowy Sandra Devlin, stood like a squat grey rock before Kay.

Kay stumbled to a stop, blinked. 'Oh, it's you, Sandra.'

'But here? Kay....'

'Hi, Sandra!' Kay said brightly, reminding herself that the best defence was a good offence, and wondering why she didn't have one at her disposal.

'But what are you doing in Rosemont?' Sandra insisted, her husky voice oddly shrill.

Kay noted that, decided that Sandra did have the good offence which was the defence. And if defence was necessary there must be a reason. Kay raised her dimpled chin, said tranquilly, 'Why, I'm leading my usual double life, that's all!'

CHAPTER 7

A Plot Presents Itself

Sandra's long dark eyes narrowed. They lingered briefly on Kay's face, then sooty false eyelashes fanned up and down and up again, obviously skimming, and cataloguing Kay's clothes.

Kay saw Sandra dismiss the double life suggestion, and observed to herself that she must remember that truth could often pass as fiction. But Sandra's reaction was understandable. Kay was hardly dressed to meet a secret lover. She wore blue jeans that were paint-stained and patched. Her white shirt was tell-tale grey, and orange-juice stained. Her grey-brown sneakers displayed holes temporarily darned by the flesh of pink toes. If there had been make-up on her face when she started out to Rosemont, the humid heat of late August had melted it all away.

Sandra on the other hand, looked quite ready for anything. She wore a sheer white dress that displayed glimmerings of tanned skin. A tiny white hat clung to her long glossy hair. Her earrings were white, as were the ribbons of her spike-heeled sandals, and her gloves. Her nose was as definitely not shiny as her mouth was definitely bright with fresh-applied lipstick.

Oh, yes, Kay thought interestedly, Sandra was certainly ready, or looked ready, for just about anything. And *anything*, to Sandra, meant a man.

It occurred to Kay, then and there, in the heat of the parking lot, that she had been remiss in not having before thought of Sandra as a heroine. Sultry, obviously. Sexy, why certainly.

Kay's fertile mind seized the germinating seed and laboured on. *She leaned over him, her long dark hair touching his bare chest. He turned her face up...*

142

But Sandra, proceeding on her own tack, and having dismissed Kay's double life admission, interrupted Kay, 'I tell you what! Let's have some lunch,' and sneaked a glance at her watch.

Kay crossly informed herself that it was time to stop thinking like Chuck Lane. There was a crisis to deal with. She clutched her manuscript, and muttered, 'Who? Me?'

'Surely.'

'But the way I look?'

Sandra shrugged her forgiveness, and her tolerance, if not her understanding.

Kay made a last lame vague attempt to escape. 'I have so many errands. I...'

Sandra insisted, emphasizing her sincerity but tugging at Kay's arm.

Doing It, wrapped, double-tied, addressed, and well-prayed over, slipped, dropped, and then hung on Kay's blue jeans. She caught the package, blessed her pants, and docilely followed Sandra off the street and into the Drug Fair.

She allowed her curiosity free rein as they settled at the soda fountain. 'And what about you, Sandra? What are you doing here? I wouldn't think it was your beat.'

'Exploring,' Sandra said so promptly that Kay knew she was hearing a demonstration of what had earlier been rehearsed. 'I've always wondered what was on the other side of the city.'

'Wondered what was in Rosemont?'

Sandra nodded. 'I guess you don't feel it, with Donnie, and all, and living the way you live, but Greenhill is so...so cloistering. Sometimes I'm afraid that if I don't get out, see how the rest of the world lives...' Long dark eyes appealed to Kay. Sooty false lashes swept up and down and up again.

'The country club,' Kay said, all agreeable tranquillity, 'the long long days...'

'You *do* understand.' There was a slight tinge of acid in Sandra's voice. She sneaked another obvious look at her wristwatch.

Still tranquil, Kay said, 'Rosemont is a funny place to start.'

Sandra shrugged.

Kay grinned, brushed red-gold bangs from her brow. Sandra's inventiveness could be strained only so far. It took only a modicum of Chuck Lane's intuition to guess that Sandra was in Rosemont to meet a man, a man that Kay would recognize, hence Sandra's insistence on dragging Kay off the parking lot and into the Drug Fair, hence her repeated glances at her watch. That Sandra's days in cloistering Greenhill were long and dull, Kay did not doubt. That boredom was the basis of many an affair of the body and heart, Kay did not doubt either.

She delicately put her assessment into words. 'I guess I'm not the only one leading a double life.'

But Sandra, busily ordering a cottage cheese salad and iced tea, pretended not to hear her.

Kay, reckless with calories, because since she had begun to share her body with Chuck Lane, she found she could afford to be, had tuna fish salad on toast, with a side order of french fried onion rings, and a double chocolate milk shake. She tackled the food with good appetite, not at all embarrassed to discover that she found herself gloating over Sandra's envious look.

Sandra, plainly dismissing her reasons for being in Rosemont, asked, 'Doing any more about that silly book project of yours?'

Kay choked on an onion ring. To her the word *book* meant *Doing It*, now on her lap, meant the portable in the kitchen, meant

Chuck Lane. She prolonged the choke until she was red in the face, but also until she could ask calmly, 'Book project, Sandra?'

'Kay! You haven't forgotten it already? You really aren't *that* scatterbrained. The P.T.A, the burn the paperbacks committee, the...'

'Oh. The CSTB.' Kay licked her fingers clean of too-sweet mayonnaise. Oh, that. Sam's project. Yes.'

'Amanda says you hardly see Sam any more.'

'I see him enough,' Kay answered, thinking of her recent scrimmage with him, and easing *Doing It,* which seemed to be afire in her lap, to a more secure position. A position in which, having checked, she was certain she had maintained its address face down.

'Then who?' Sandra was asking.

'Who what?'

'Who *are* you seeing, Kay dear?'

Kay moaned silently. It was impossible for her, ever, to credit the degree to which her friends emphasized the need for masculine attentions. She couldn't credit it. She didn't want them. She took a deep breath, plunged. 'I see you, Sandra. And

Donnie, and Amanda, and James. There's also Margery and Dick. Not to mention Mr Fairbanks and Mr Avis, and...'

'A really exciting lot.' Sandra's husky voice deepened with disapproval, but her long dark eyes seemed unaccountably pleased. 'And,' she went on, 'You're terribly skinny, too.'

'Terrible, isn't it,' Kay grinned, suddenly enjoying herself.

'Amanda's right. You ought to do something. And wait until she hears how you're rigged out.'

'Just errands after all,' Kay deprecated. 'And I am actually so busy somehow...'

'Abnormal,' Sandra said silkily, 'the way you seem to avoid having anything serious to do with a man.'

'I don't want to,' Kay told her. Firm voice, firm heart. Thinking of Earl supplied the concrete. Besides, there were already enough men in her life. Donnie, James, Dick, Ralph, Sam...and...oh, yes, most important, Chuck Lane. Chuck Lane himself.

'And if you want the male point of view, well, there's Michael, too. He's concerned.'

'He is?'

'Women who are too rigid in their ideas

end up on the shelf. That's the male point of view.'

'Where I want to be,' Kay grinned.

She knew for certain now what the next one would be. *Bored.* She could see the title page, the Chuck Lane byline. Chapter 1. Oh, yes, definitely. *Bored.*

She could have hugged Sandra. Instead, she gulped her milk shake, said, 'I have to go now..'

Sandra glanced at her watch. 'Oh, you mustn't rush off.'

'Errands in my double life,' Kay said serenely, and dropped a dollar on the counter, and clutched the manuscript closer, as she rose and walked away.

The Drug Fair had a huge paperback section. Kay paused before it, knowing that Sandra was anxiously watching her, and wondering what man Sandra hoped Kay wouldn't see. But, seeing Chuck Lane's books, lined up and neatly arranged, she forgot about Sandra, and her clandestine affair. *The Hot Stars, Loving, Adventuring.* Kay basked in sheer pure joy. Even with Sandra watching anxiously, there were some small pleasures Kay could not deny herself. A single copy of *Hot Stars* was out of line. She automatically righted it. She took a last fond look, feasting on heady fare, then hurried outside.

The post office was as crowded as always. Even so, Kay was hailed by a 'Hi there, Mrs Lane,' from a grinning clerk.

Once again she wished for that happy anonymity which she imagined could be, ought to be, found somewhere in some happy time, but seemed never to be where she was. It did not occur to her that a small, curvaceous girl, with reddish curls and amber eyes, a girl wearing snug blue jeans, a snug white shirt, swinging along in sneakers, girl with a ready smile and a ready dimple, rarely moved unnoticed through meadows of male interest.

She sidled to her box, having cast a last careful look at the door, through which she saw an overflow of on-sale lawn mowers and bales of peat, but no slender white form. Sandra had departed for wherever she had planned to depart to.

Relieved, Kay withdrew her mail. Five letters. One from Britanica Company, Inc. She wondered what Galen Maradick would have to say. Four others. Unfamiliar return addresses. Not ads. She had become adept at spotting them. Not ads? Then fan letters? She considered them uneasily. But there was no time then to investigate. She stuffed everything into her purse, and went to mail *Doing It*.

Sandra had not departed. She stood among the on-sale lawn mowers, nervously smoothing her white gloves. 'Done?' she asked brightly, and at Kay's unwilling nod, 'Let's shop.'

'I don't have time.'

Sandra pouted, 'I can't see why.' And trailed Kay to the emerald-green car. 'It's lovely, Kay. Such a nice present to yourself. I just don't see how you do it.'

The letters in Kay's purse seemed to swell, grow, burst into flame. She clutched the hot plastic in cold hands. 'I'd better get along, Sandra,' and then, inspired, 'Amanda said she'd be over.'

'You're up to something,' Sandra said, narrowing her long dark eyes. 'I've had the feeling all along. You can see Amanda any time. So...' Her throaty voice became a whisper. 'We're old friends, Kay. You can tell me.' So saying, Sandra's long dark eyes slipped past Kay's shirted shoulder, and widened, and her slim body, suddenly awkward, moved in a small circle.

Kay, automatically adjusting to the new

position, realized that she was being maneouvred. But she grinned. 'Tell you? Tell you what? Unless you mean about my double life.'

Sandra tried to look reproachful. But her attention had wandered, and her slim hands nervously twisted her white gloves.

Kay took advantage of the unknown diversion. Feeling decidedly joyful, she got into the emerald-green car, and waved at Sandra, and drove off with that sweet nonchalance that only a new hard-topped convertible can bestow. Moments later, all nonchalance gone, she stalled.

Behind her stood willowy Sandra, still nervously twisting white gloves in nervous hands.

Before her, seated in a parked car, face turned away, but with a suspiciously familiar looking sandy head, was a man. A man who could be, who looked like, who definitely was, her ex-husband, Earl.

She managed, proud of steady hands and cool head, to get her car started on her third try. Nonchalance redonned, but frayed as an old coat, she started out for Greenhill.

Amanda's baby-blue convertible was parked in the lane.

Kay muttered an unladylike oath. She would, she told herself, have to learn that the lies she told had a way of becoming truth.

Living proof was Amanda. She stood in the doorway, tapping a shiny patent-leather toe.

The letters in Kay's purse seemed about to explode. She longed to defuse them. But she slipped from the car, purse clutched tightly under her arm.

'That,' Amanda said, blue-green eyes full of pitying disapproval, 'now that is quite an outfit. Suppose you met someone you knew? Or wanted to know. Suppose someone just happened to...'

For *someone* say a man, Kay thought. Aloud she said, '*You* look lovely, really.'

Amanda preened, acknowledging the compliment. Then, 'Margery is inside, getting the boys a snack.'

Kay's heart sank. She made a lunge for the kitchen, amber eyes raised anxiously to the treasure chest cookie bin on the refrigerator. It squatted there, big, brown, bound in brass, and unopened.

'What's the matter with you?' Margery asked, pouring milk into Kay's best glasses, and into puddles on the tabletop.

152

Heart rising to its accustomed place, Kay greeted her sister, her two small nephews, and then, with a muttered 'Excuse me, I've got to go,' she fled to the bathroom, taking her purse with her.

With the door firmly locked behind her, the voices of relatives a fading chorus, she at last opened her mail. Galen Maradick wrote:

Dear Chuck,

Please, as soon as you receive this, call me (212-111-1111) about some really important news. I find that you are a very hard person to get in touch with by phone. In fact, I find that you're impossible. We've had a whole squad of secretaries working on it for three days. Are you a hermit? Who ever heard of anybody in this day and age, especially anybody in a place called Rosemont, who doesn't have a phone? The really important news? Your next book (on the basis of your projection of Doing It, *and assuming that it comes out okay) could very definitely be a hard-cover sale, kiddo. How do you like that? The same stuff you usually do, of course, but take your time. I mean, get started right away but take your time. Make it deeper, smoother, and with the always good, you-know-what and*

153

plenty of it. Money? Double the 15 to 30. Possibilities? Unlimited. So call, will you? And we need a biography, so send it right away.

Warmest regards, Chuck Galen

Kay choked back a muted yip of delight. Her widening amber eyes skimmed the letter a second time. *Dear Chuck.* Yes. *Hard-cover sale.* Yes. *Call me immediately.* Yes. *Warmest regards, Chuck.* Yes, yes, oh, yes. She read the letter one more time. She stroked the crisp paper. Definitely real. Yes. She folded it into her purse.

Amanda called, 'Kay, sweetheart, what is it? Are you all right?'

Kay quickly flushed the commode. 'Coming.' she called, and took the other four envelopes from her purse.

She went over them quickly. One said that any woman married to Chuck Lane was a lucky woman, and if her husband, the correspondent's, were like that, instead of like he was, she would be a lucky woman and a happy woman. And if Chuck Lane wasn't already married, would he please contact the correspondent at... From there it went on to make a variety of unseemly offers.

The second was shorter. Thus:

Dear Chuck Lane,
Who can believe anybody anywhere, can act
like those people you write about. I've looked
in three atlases and I can't find a town named
Tonnerton. Please hurry up and say where it
is so I can get myself to it right away.

The third was a threat. Chuck Lane was to be sued for eight million dollars, having divulged the private life of the undersigned. That was invasion of privacy, and nobody, not Chuck Lane or anybody else, had the right to do that.

The fourth began fairly reasonably. To wit:

Dear Mr Lane,
You're a pretty good writer, all right. I like
just about everything you have to say. Only
you're not realistic enough. Quit closing the
bedroom door and pulling up the sheets. Keep
the door wide open, throw the sheets on the
floor where they belong.

Kay sighed. Shades of Galen Maradick. She read on. Her eyes widened. She gasped. Following that annoying, but still reasonable comment, there was a string of obscene words. Words that Kay had seen in print, but never in letters addressed to her. But these, she thought edgily, were not addressed to her. They were for Chuck Lane's eyes.

Amanda shouted, 'Kay! Sweetheart!'

She slipped the letters into her purse, the purse into the formica vanity under the sink. She rinsed her mouth before she realized what she was doing, and told herself she would have done better to rinse her eyes. She hurried into the kitchen in time to hear Margery say, full of woe, '...and all I did was put my feet on his back. Where the pyjamas meet. Just snuggled them up against him. He's got soft skin there, and it's warm. And he got up out of bed and slammed into the other room, and...'

Amanda gave a ladylike but thoroughly disapproving snort.

Margery turned brown eyes full of disenchantment on Kay. 'What should I do?'

Amanda's snort turned into a sharp, 'Your sister Kay is hardly an authority on men. And that, sweetheart,' she went on, turning to Kay, '...is why I stopped by.'

'Oh?' Kay braced.

'Sam visited me last night.'

'Oh?' Kay repeated, bracing further.

'And what about Ralph Parlmeyer?' Margery put in. 'Really, Kay. It's abnormal.'

'A matter of taste,' Kay brought out, dividing her answer equally between mother and sister.

'When a woman wants a man, she finds the right one,' Amanda announced.

That, Kay thought, was certainly true of Amanda. She had a string of too-young men to amuse her. The latest being by all reports, the parking lot attendant at the country club, a husky twenty-year-old named Carl Hessler, whose ability to express himself, Kay suspected, was limited to, 'Hunh! Hunh?' and 'Cool!'

'She finds the right one,' Margery echoed. Rising, she gathered her two small dozing sons to her, gathered them without much warmth, and asked drearily, 'But suppose she's still so tied down that...'

Amanda rose, too. 'I'm off to the club.'

'A big help,' Margery said.

'I expect my grown daughters to be able to figure out certain things for themselves.' Amanda departed, trailing unseen scarves of icy disapproval.

Margery followed, dragging two tiny boys.

Kay went along. She was waving goodbye, her small curved body weak with relief, when, from inside, she heard the ringing of the phone.

CHAPTER 8

A Crusader Comes

She stood quite still, hoping that the ringing would stop, that whoever waited at the other end of the telephone wires would give up and go away.

She stood quite still, oppressed by hot August air, and tried to concentrate on the slivers of gold streaked on the lilac hedge by the glaring sun. But the commanding mesmerizing, irritating sound went on and on. A cardinal gave up and fluttered away. A starling gave up and silenced its chatter. She finally gave up, and hurried inside.

She caught up the phone in time to hear, 'Well, goddam it, don't any of these silly women ever stay home?'

'I do,' she said brightly. 'And furthermore it is against the law to swear over the phone. If swearing comes under the category of obscene language, that is. See the telephone directory, page...' She stopped. She didn't know the page number. Besides, she felt that she had avenged herself for the unwanted summons.

The voice that replied was deep, clearly male, drawling, with a hint of laughter, and totally unfamiliar. It said, 'Excuse the language. I'll check the obscene bit later. Right now, I want to...'

'Who is this?' she asked, and was suddenly cold, struck by the frightening thought that Galen Maradick, Britanica Company, Inc., had managed to track her down. She summoned fortitude to accept whatever came.

The deep, drawling voice said, 'Mrs Barrenger, this is Jonathan Williams. I'm editor of the *Greenhill Sentinel*.'

'Jonathan Williams?' Not Galen Maradick then. Not Britanica Company Inc. She became effusive in her relief. 'Oh, yes, Mr Williams. I *have* heard of you.'

'You're a faithful subscriber, I hope.'

'Certainly.' Bemused, wondering why that deep, drawling, and totally unfamiliar voice should make peculiar prickles prickle along her arms, she didn't admit that she had been conned into a three year subscription by Sam Golden's oldest son, and that the *Greenhill Sentinel* went into the trash each week, unread, and even un-folded.

'I'm hot on the trail of some big news,' Jonathan said. 'And you're the only one that can help me, Mrs Barrenger.'

'I am?'

'The contests.'

'Contests?' She decided that the prickles prickling along her arms, the odd weakness in her legs, were both symptoms of fatigue. She decided that Jonathan Williams had a very good voice, a very male voice, which meant, no doubt, that he was sixty-five, stout, bald, and afflicted, in some way she had not yet discovered.

'The contests you've won,' Jonathan said. 'I'd like to know all about them. My readers would be very interested. And, to tell you the truth, so am I. Somehow I had the idea, obviously I was all wrong, wasn't I, that such things are things of the past.'

'You mean the contests I won,' Kay said weakly, and cursed the gods who had supplied her with that particular lie. 'Oh. I see.'

'Now then.' Jonathan's deep, drawling voice became brisk. Pencils rattled. Paper rustled. 'How many contests have you entered? What were they? How many have you actually won? What were the exact amounts of the prizes? Also, I know my readers would want to know...'

Kay said, 'Just a minute please. Before you go on, I ought to tell you that I'm not interested in having my name in the *Greenhill Sentinel*.'

'You aren't?' He sounded totally confounded.

'I'm not.'

'But what you've done is news, Mrs Barrenger.'

'My mother always told me that a lady only has her name in the papers three times in her life. When she's born. When she marries. And when she...'

'When she is divorced?'

Kay's sudden appreciative grin did not warm her cold voice saying, 'And when she dies, Mr Williams.'

'Your mother?'

'That's right.'

His voice was suddenly silky, sinister

but silky. Kay told herself that he must be speaking through gritted false teeth.

He said, 'Your mother is, I believe, Mrs ah...now what is it? I can never remember the first name, but...'

'Mrs James Mason?' Kay supplied.

'Yes. That's it. Thanks. Mrs James Mason is your mother. Right?'

'Yes. And...'

He went on, sinister silkiness even more noticeable 'She called me this morning, Mrs Barrenger. That's how I knew about your winning the contests.'

'Oh.'

'So you see...'

Kay saw. She suddenly choked on thick hot waves of rage. Small flames flared in her amber eyes. Her red-gold bangs crackled electrically. The prickles prickling along her arms were unbearable; the odd weakness in her legs was unbearable. So was his silky, drawling voice that seemed to imply he saw her, daughter of Amanda Mason, as a stout chocolate-nibbling matron who longed for attention. The fact that she had been caught in what she had thought to be a clever lie was most unbearable of all.

Raging, she reached for cool, at least for

haughty, amusement. 'I can't talk to you right now. It's not convenient.'

'Oh? Why not, Mrs Barrenger?'

'The house...' Reaching for, but not quite reaching, either cool or haughty amusement, she blurted, 'I, I can't. The house...I think it's burning down.' And then, with an extremely realistic yip of anguish, she slammed the phone into its cradle.

She turned away, brushing both small hands together in a firm, 'Well, that's over with' gesture, and headed for the pantry, the portable, and work.

She didn't make it.

The front door slammed.

Donnie yelled, 'Mom, I'm home. Rick's mother says can I have supper with Rick at their house?'

Swallowing an eager, almost-uttered cry of, 'Certainly!' Kay considered. Rick's mother had had Rick and Donnie for most of the day. Still their house was just next door. When Donnie palled they could easily point him toward home. And one did not, Kay assured herself, refuse small favours. She returned to the hall. 'You may have dinner at Rick's.'

But Donnie wasn't listening. He ducked

his head. His ears seemed to point. His eyes certainly brightened. 'Say, listen! They're coming this way!' He did a fawn leap through the open door.

Sirens. Bells.

Distant. Closer, Rising. Falling. Rising. Rising. Deafening. Dying...dying...

Kay gaped. She went outside.

There she turned. She gave her house an unbelieving look. She stared. She sniffed. She swung back to bestow an even more unbelieving look at the two fire trucks that had roared to a stop, sirens whining and fading. And as men leaped to the ground, spun pulleys, dragged hoses, and shouted, a small tan sedan bounced around a corner, skidded with tyres shrieking, and rattled to a halt just ahead of them.

'Mo-ther?' Donnie cried, all delight and bewilderment, 'Mo-ther! Are we burning?'

The firemen charged up the walk, thrust her and Donnie aside. They hauled great throbbing snakes of hose, and swinging axes, and trumpeted unintelligible orders.

Rick's mother, and Rick, and assorted children, watched from their own front yard.

All that, and Kay stood and stared and shivered, and finally, just as her door was about to be breached, she shrilled, 'Just a minute! I'm afraid there's been a terrible mistake!'

At that there began a nightmare interrogation.

It began, 'Say, what do you mean?'

Some time during the middle of it when Kay, hopeless, and wordless, allowed her ridiculous no-explanation to die in helpless feminine tears, she noticed that the driver of the small tan sedan had left it to linger at the edges of the group, to linger and listen and shake his head disapprovingly.

The interrogation at last came to an end with a disappointed, 'Well, if you're sure there's no fire,' and a doubtful look at the calm, smokeless, flameless house. And finally, with a, 'Say, lady, you know what the penalty is for turning in a false alarm?'

'I did not! And I do not!' Miraculously Kay's tears dried. Previously absent fire suddenly glowed in her amber eyes.

The driver of the small tan sedan unobtrusively made his way from the fringes of the group to its centre. He carried an extremely obtrusive, and professional-looking camera. He was tall, and lean. He had wildly dishevelled hair, cut short but prone to curl. It was that off-shade of russet that bespoke a childhood of fights. He might have outgrown being called Carrot-top, but he certainly hadn't outgrown the aggressive jaw that went with it.

He said, level hazel eyes avoiding Kay's hard stare, 'The lady doesn't know about the alarm, Chief. I'm afraid that was my fault. Strictly a misunderstanding.'

Scowls became smiles, the false alarm forgotten. 'Say, when did you get here, Mr Williams?'

Soon, with pictures taken, apologies accepted, the firemen departed.

As they did, Rick's mother, Rick, and the assorted children, went indoors. Donnie charged after them only to return immediately.

Rick's mother had decided Donnie ought to remain at home to keep Kay company.

Kay said she wasn't really surprised, and registered his disappointment with only half attention. The rest of it was centred on Jonathan Williams, who had turned out to be neither short, nor fat, nor bald, nor wearing false teeth. Remaining after the firemen's departure, he approached her now. One hand held the camera, the other made smoothing motions that ruffled even further his already ruffled hair.

'You,' he said, 'you must be Mrs Barrenger. What an extraordinary thing to do.'

She noticed that his deep, drawling voice, no longer soft and pleasant, no longer even silky, still made prickles prickle on her arms. She noticed an odd weakness in her legs. She found herself irrationally damning blue jeans and sneakers.

It was quite natural that she should have an academic interest in all such phenomena, but she decided to consider them at some other time. She made a neat military turn, and started towards her door.

'It just doesn't make sense,' Jonathan said. 'Unless...'

She turned back. 'You guessed it, Mr Williams. Unless I didn't want to talk to you. And I still don't.'

'So you said the house was burning down?' He didn't wait for an answer. 'Of course. Perfectly logical. I suppose.'

She did not care to deal with his sarcasm. She headed for the door again. But there was Donnie, disconsolately toeing the walk. She made another turn, prepared to call him in. She found herself swallowing the shout.

Jonathan's lean face was inches from

hers. His hazel eyes, glowered at her from under imposingly-dark straight brows. 'You ought to have more respect for the press!'

She summoned slender resources. 'I am sorry. But I did think, while I was talking to you, that I smelled smoke. It was just imagination, of course. So I forgot about it. And then...'

'Imagination.' He plainly did not accept that, but he just as plainly decided not to belabour the point. He went on, 'About the contests, Mrs Barrenger...'

She summoned completely-depleted resources. 'I am, as a matter of principle, opposed to personal publicity.' It sounded pretty good to her ears.

But not to his. He demanded, 'Then shouldn't you avoid engaging yourself in ridiculous activities?'

She stared at him, the prickles prickling harder than ever along her arms, and decided that he really was a very odd man. 'Ridiculous activities?'

'That P.T.A committee. The one to check on those books. Now, Mrs Barrenger...' He stopped, eyed her narrowly. Then, 'Listen, you aren't kidding me, are you? You are Kay Barrenger?'

168

'I am.'

'That's funny,' he mused.

'It is?'

'Women's magazines contests. Committees to burn books. I mean, it just doesn't fit. The way I thought you were, the picture I had of you, yes, that. Sure. But the way you are.'

'We are not going to burn books,' she snapped. 'I wouldn't take part in that kind of a...'

'Then what are you going to do? After you see about them, what then?'

'We haven't decided.'

'Who's we?'

'The people on the committee.'

His voice went silky. 'You mean Sam Golden? And what's her name? Mrs Planter? You think they haven't decided?'

'I am chairman,' Kay said.

'So it's true.' Jonathan shook his head sadly. 'Listen, what do you think such committees are for? Investigate first. Yes. Yes. That's the programme all right. And after the investigation...'

She opened her mouth to reply.

'Never mind, Mrs Barrenger. I can see that appearances are deceiving. Even if you don't look it, you are that kind of a...'

'Dried out old bat?' she suggested.

He didn't demure. He said, 'I hate to see you make such a fool of yourself.'

She would have answered him if she could have thought of anything to say.

He didn't wait. He jerked his head at her, squared his shoulders and went down to his car. As he drove away, it made rude backfiring sounds of contempt.

She resisted an urge to stick out her tongue. He was plainly a man who needed looking after. She had noticed that he wore one white sock, one pale grey one. His trousers required a good pressing. His shirt had missed a button.

All things considered she was delighted that he was not her responsibility.

Donnie came up to announce what had been obvious for some time. 'Rick's mother didn't want me after all. And they all went inside.' And then, 'Why is everybody leaving, Mom?'

'Because we're outcasts,' Kay told him. 'Let's celebrate with hamburgers.'

But the fire engines, and the perfidy of Rick's mother, had been too much for him. He didn't want hamburgers. He didn't want to go to bed. He didn't want Kay to do her practising that night. With the lights out, at last, he became conversational. He rehashed the oddities of the firemen, the strange visit of the photographer. At last he announced, 'What we really need is a man around this house.'

'Oh, no, we don't,' Kay said.

'But why not?'

'Because I don't like men.'

'But I'm a man,' Donnie cried indignantly, and at the same time, his thumb crept toward his mouth.

Too late, Kay saw her error and sought to mend it. 'You're my son. That's entirely different.'

He parlayed the worn-out subject into a ten minute delay, and fell asleep before he had used them up.

She closed his door gently, leaned there, breathing hard for a moment. But only for a moment. Then, straightening her shoulders, amber eyes ablaze with excitement, she retrieved her purse from the bathroom vanity and headed for the kitchen.

Portable arranged, coffee poured, pencils and erasers lined up, she settled happily at the table.

Not so happily, she read once more the letter from Britanica Company Inc. Not that the joyful expectation outlined in it troubled her. Oh, no. It raised her to the peaks of euphoria. But Galen Maradick's breezy request for a call, a biography, suggested distinct possibilities of trouble ahead. He was trying to make Chuck Lane her whole life. And that was decidedly too much.

She whipped white paper, carbon, yellow paper, together, and whipped the set into the portable. She considered for a scant moment before pounding out a peremptory letter. Thus:

Dear Gale:

Thank you for the good news. I will do the best I can, and if you do, then maybe the next book will sell hardcover. As for the rest... I have no phone. I see no reason to call you. I see no reason for supplying a biography. I want to be left alone, except to be sent contracts, and cheques, and contracts and more cheques.

Truly,
Chuck Lane

She addressed the envelope quickly. As she wrote Attn: Galen Maradick, she suddenly wondered if there really was a

Galen Maradick. After all, there wasn't any Chuck Lane. It could, she thought, become quite interesting. Two phantoms writing to each other...

She didn't have time to pursue it.

There was a knock at the door.

She gave the littered table a wild glance, then crumpled a dish towel and flung it over the letter to Galen and his to her. It wasn't much, but seemed the best she could do.

She found Jonathan Williams on her door step. He gave her a big warm smile. He drawled, 'I thought I'd stop back for a few minutes. If you have time now.'

It occurred to her that newspapermen had reputations for aggressiveness.

She noted that his russet hair was combed, its tendency to curl somewhat subdued.

She saw that his socks matched, that he looked brushed and steamed and eager.

She felt prickles prickle along her arms, and a weakness in her legs.

She managed a cool, 'Sorry. I'm busy.'

His big warm smile shrank and dimmed. He thrust three books into her hand. 'Okay. You're busy. But take some time to read these, Mrs Barrenger. You read them, and

173

you'll see what a mistake you're making in being on that ridiculous committee.'

Her fingers closed around *Adventuring, The Hot Stars, Loving.* She accepted the books, and held them, and gave Jonathan a blank look.

Misunderstanding, he went on patiently, 'The committee about the paperbacks. Remember, Mrs Barrenger? You're the chairwoman, and...'

'You want me to read them?' she asked.

'I do. They won't hurt you.' His deep drawling voice became silky and bitter at the same time. 'They might even do you some good.'

She said, 'All right. I'll read them. Good night,' and slammed the door.

CHAPTER 9

Blow-Out

It soothed Kay slightly to make lists.

Dawn of a mid-September day seemed as good a time as any for soothing.

She wrote:

Bored! Then, *Grocery* shop. And, *Rosemont*. Next, *Donnie's underpants*. Fifth, *Check Thespian meeting*.

She realized that she had omitted laundry, but didn't add it. She told herself that she was soothed. There was no use in allowing herself only five hours of sleep a night, of rising before dawn, if she didn't go to work. She yawned.

Donnie said plaintively from the doorway. 'Mo-ther! Are you going to start practising now?' He regarded her from sarcastic blue eyes that reminded her more of Earl than she cared for.

'I guess you can't sleep anymore, can you?'

'It's the first day.'

'No. I guess you can't.'

'If first grade is for pretty big boys, then I don't see why I can't have a two-wheel bike.'

'Your logic is impeccable.' She waited for him to demand a definition.

He said, 'What?'

That sounded, not like Earl, but suspiciously like Kay herself. She knew the tone, and the refusal to accept that led to pretended deafness. She didn't bother to reply.

She poured orange juice, milk, toasted three slices of bread. She dumped dry cereal in a bowl, added a handful of raisins, as bribe or bait. She said, 'Brush teeth, comb hair, and return, pretty big boy. I'll get your clothes out for you.'

'All done.' He sat at the table. Then, 'Are you going to take me to school?'

'I hadn't planned to.'

'Good.'

'Are you sure, Donnie?' He suddenly seemed smaller, younger, than she had thought. After all, it was four long blocks. Vocabulary was no defence against speeding cars...

'Mo-ther!' In a tone of indignant outrage.

She gathered that he was sure, but hid her relief that he was the self-reliant brave, absolutely unsurprisable child she had assessed him to be. However, the thought of the speeding cars still troubled her.

Later, when he was ready, he brushed a kiss on the air near her cheek, and started off. Her relief changed to grief. She *was* not the self-reliant, brave, absolutely unsur-prisable *mother* that she had assessed herself to be. She threw herself into activity.

When the household chores were done, kitchen, bath, and Donnie's room, she decided to change from pyjamas to pants before her trip to the Greenhill shopping centre. One leg into faded jeans, she found herself thinking of Jonathan Williams. He put out a pretty good newspaper. She had read it carefully, cover to cover, the first Friday after his two visits. She had choked, remembering how solemnly she promised to read Chuck Lane's books. Jonathan Williams, editor, publisher, owner. And *he* called *her* ridiculous! She had read it carefully, cover to cover, the second Friday after his two visits. There was no mention of contests; she did not see her name. She did see that the *Greenhill Sentinel's* offices were located above the barbershop in the shopping centre. Without thinking about it at all, she withdrew one leg from faded jeans, and burrowed into her closet...

She wore a green plaid transitional print, in honour of mid-September, she told herself. It was new. A little nothing that she had treated herself to when she received the first advance on *Doing It*. She wore spike-heeled shoes, another small treat. They took her briskly past the barbershop and through the grocery. They marched her past the barbershop again and into Boys' World. She bought Donnie four pairs of underpants, and a huge pencil box, attache case cum laude, of red plastic. It seemed to her just what the well-equipped first grader should own. Once again she passed the barbershop. Beyond it, Mr Avis waved hopefully and sociably from his window. She went in.

'Fine September day,' he beamed, approving brown eyes peering at her from pads of pink flesh.

'Lovely,' she agreed, and headed for the drug counter, which took her past the paperback racks. She paused there, as if one of the bright covers had suddenly caught her eye. In fact, nothing caught her eye. Her pose of idle interest fell away from her. Her amber eyes swept up and down, across and back. Where was *Adventuring*? Where *The Hot Stars*? Where *Loving*? Mr Avis watched her interestedly, asked, 'Checking up on me, hunh?'

'What?' She continued her search.

'The committee.' He laughed. 'Everybody knows about it, Mrs Barrenger.'

'Committee?' No *Adventuring*, no *Hot Stars*, no *Loving*. She resisted an impulse to kick over the paperback rack.

'*Your* committee, Mrs Barrenger. The one to investigate those books. I ought to have guessed, that day you bought them. Still, who'd ever think...'

'I was just looking for something to read,' she told him, edging away from the rack.

'To read, and after that...' He made a throat-cutting gesture. 'Only guess what happened?' His beer fat jiggled all over with a deep laugh. 'Your Sam Golden mentioned an author and a book, and he sold me out.'

'What?' Kay demanded.

'Sold me out! And every place else in Greenhill. That's what happens, Mrs Barrenger. You tell people they can't, and they will.'

Kay went straight to the drug counter. She bought a bottle of aspirin. She departed, with Mr Avis, trailing her to the door, still assuring her that her committee was the best advertising a book ever had.

She passed the barbershop again, carefully not looking at the upstairs windows. She had heard as much about the CSTB as she cared to hear. The bright green plaid seemed dull, the waist too loose, the hem too low. She went home.

Groceries stored.

Laundry sudsing in the washer.

Celebration cake for Donnie, a boy didn't enter first grade every day, in the oven.

Portable on the table. A stack of yellow paper. Erasers, pencils, ashtray. Coffee perking.

Kay, comfortable in jeans, took a long deep breath, murmured, 'Yes, Sandra. I remember, Sandra. I don't know if I can make it.'

Sandra's throaty voice seemed somehow strident on the phone. 'But it's the first meeting. Thespians needs you. Who else'll do the costumes?'

'Oh, I'll do them. One of them anyhow.'

'And if I come over earlier, we'll have time for coffee, for a chat.'

'Better not. That's when I'm going to be doing laundry.'

'I'll be happy to pick you up.'

'I can get there, Sandra.'

Sandra sulky, 'Oh, all right, Kay. See you tonight then.'

'Tonight,' Kay echoed, and wondered what all that was in aid of. A new conference between Amanda and Sandra? An additional affirmation that something had to be done about Kay? Or...and this was more likely... Sandra now operating on her own. *Adventuring* wrapped in purple towel in Sandra's guest powder room. Had that been a subtle Sandra way of announcing to Kay that Sandra KNEW? Sandra in Rosemont, nervously twisting white gloves, attired in glorious white, and Earl, dark head turned carefully away. But that was something else again.

Kay informed herself that she was not going to waste time considering Sandra's games. She snapped two sheets of yellow paper into the portable, and typed, *Bored by Chuck Lane.*

It was an excellent title, she decided with a slight nod at the absent Sandra. And so, Starrleigh and Earl—

But her fingers hung over the keyboard.

Stuck.

Stuck?

Impossible.

She banged out *Chapter 5.* Yes. *Bored by Chuck Lane. Chapter 5.*

In the past few weeks, since hearing from Galen Maradick, she had worked hard. There were four sizzling chapters, but deeper, smoother, realer. Very definitely realer. She was going to make it, and fifteen hundred dollars would become three thousand dollars, and...

And she sighed. More trouble ahead. What about *that* contract? What about *that* money? What about Galen Maradick?

She told herself to stop burying her head in piles of irrelevancies. She told herself to go to work. Her hands hung limply over the stubborn keyboard.

She swore and gave up and gave in. She took out the shiny yellow-covered paperback that had become talisman and catalyst. She opened it at random, and read:

His hips bounced, fluttered, socked, circled, rammed...

That was quite enough. She closed the book, and went back to the portable.

Chapter 5. *'Don't you know anything new?' Starrleigh groaned. Earl didn't answer her. He considered that everything new had been tried out by Adam and Eve in the Garden of Eden, and that the chances were that whatever had been new then had become old by now. Besides, he was the victim of certain anatomical and imaginative limitations. And quite satisfied with them, and himself. Or would be in a little while. Meantime, he pinioned her writhing hips with his weight,*

*and gasped, 'It's always new, Starrleigh.'
'Oh, hurry,' she cried, 'please, hurry hurry,'
but that made him laugh, and the laugh slowed
him, which was good, good for both of them in
spite of her whispered protest. He was buried in
her, plunging, plunging, and she arched up to
him, her hands clawed, raking his back...*

Kay arrived ten minutes late for the
Thespian meeting. She was breathless,
uncombed, unbrushed, unmade-up, and
unprepared.

Mostly she was unprepared for the sight
of Margery, dressed in a snug black suit,
snugly sitting with Ralph Parlmeyer. But
she was equally unprepared for Sandra's
suspicious, 'Amanda called you five times
this afternoon and you were out.'

Kay had heard the phone, simply ignored
it. She had decided that Chuck Lane never
bothered with answering inopportune calls.
He had the will power to ignore them. She
asked tranquilly, 'What did my mother
want?'

'That's a surprise. So I won't tell you.'

Kay didn't pursue it.

The meeting proceeded through its first
order of business, a discussion of what play
the Thespians would do that season. The

newest member, Ralph Parlmeyer, rose. He had a list of suggestions. He took his big pipe from his wide smile, and presented them in his most sober Jersey truck drivers' diction. It took him ten minutes.

Kay hoped he lived off Martinis and pastel cigarettes while he worked on the play. She stopped trying to listen. Somewhere in the middle of *Bored, Chapter 6*, the meeting came to an end. Kay didn't hear that.

Sandra nudged her. 'Going to sit here all night?'

'What?'

'Really, dear,' Sandra said sweetly. 'You're so...abstracted these days. Have you thought of a tonic?'

Margery suggested coffee. Sandra agreed. Kay, clinging to *Chapter 6*, refused. Ralph hugging Margery to his barrel chest, told Kay something in a significant voice. She translated it into, 'I've been thinking of you a lot lately,' but didn't translate the significance.

She spread a grin between the three of them, and made her escape, still in the middle of *Bored, Chapter 6*.

She was abruptly, unpleasantly, interrupted.

A block from home, with her house lights visible through the leaves of autumn-touched trees, she heard a sudden terrifying blast. As its deafening echoes died, the emerald-green car jerked sideways, and skidded, and lurched into a drainage ditch.

When the spinning night settled again, Kay found herself rigid, frozen to the wheel. The blow-out didn't matter. What had happened to the new car didn't matter. But what had *almost* happened to Kay mattered very much.

She shivered, wondering what was the reason for her irresponsible behaviour. She had known the complications, seen them, understood them. Not the fine print in the contracts, which paled to invisibility, to nothingness, beside the real problem. Not the unnerving fan mail. Nor Galen Maradick's increasing personal interest. All that was nothing, nothing. But Donnie...Donnie had to be protected. The money she was saving for him in an account belonging to Chuck Lane was for his future. Not the bank's, not the state's. For Donnie. If the car had slewed into a tree, instead of into a drainage ditch...if she had been thrown out, instead of frozen to the wheel...

By the time she had walked home, phoned the garage to take care of replacing the blown-out tyre, she had made up her mind.

Aker and Devlin had a suite of offices. It was impressively decorated with sound-proofing pale blue carpets and heavy drapes at all-glass walls. It exuded an aura of secretiveness and security which was just what Kay wanted.

Chuck Lane had intruded into her life to a point where she began to feel there was hardly room for herself. If she didn't find out how to handle him, he would end up handling her. Thus, bright and early, dressed appropriately in a black suit and a white blouse, she had come to consult Mr Aker himself.

It wasn't the first time. He had, with plain-spoken reservations, handled her divorce from Earl. Straight-laced, honest, a man to be trusted to keep secrets. That was Sandra's father.

Kay was prematurely relieved as she tiptoed across the blue carpet to the receptionist's desk. She would soon hand all her troubles to Mr Aker, and he would deal with them one by one, and end up filing them safely away.

Good.

But, she was informed by the dimpled receptionist, Mr Aker was away on vacation, and wouldn't be back for a month. So sorry, really, but it just couldn't be helped, could it? Particularly since Mrs Barrenger hadn't called ahead for an appointment.

That was a simple detail Kay had forgotten. It became less simple when Michael Devlin opened a frosted door, said, 'Kay! I thought I heard your voice. What are you doing here?'

What good was all that sound-proofing? she asked herself crossly, but said aloud, 'Oh, I just stopped to see Mr Aker. Now I find him on vacation.'

Michael's pleasant, golf-tanned face re-arranged itself. He frowned importantly. 'No trouble with Earl, I trust?'

'Oh, no.'

'Then?'

'It can wait.'

Michael was beside her, guiding her, not to the outer door, but back, back, back into his own office. 'Now, listen, don't run away,' he told her. 'I'm sure I can help you.'

Guided, led, captured, she thought, she found herself sitting beside a desk just as imposing as she remembered Mr Aker's desk to be. And on it, lovely cover glowing under the light, was a copy of *Adventuring*.

She looked at it and couldn't look away. Not immediately. And not in time.

Michael grinned. 'Home work in the office, I guess you'd call it. Getting pointers maybe, and some amusement. Everybody's been talking about it since your committee got itself started. Sold out every place. You'll never guess where I finally found it. Wrapped in towels, yes, that's right, in our downstairs bathroom.'

'In towels?' she echoed faintly.

'The maid.' Michael grinned. 'She's been spending hours at a time in there, Sandra was wondering what the hell was going on. Hours in there, reading it.'

Kay considered means of escape, saw none.

'But that's not why you're here,' Michael went on. 'Now then...'

It was, she saw absolutely no use. She would never be able to leave Aker and Devlin without telling Michael why she had come there.

She drew a long slow breath. She twisted

her hands in her lap. She averted her eyes. From *Adventuring*. From Michael.

He waited expectantly. It was obvious that he was prepared for a shocker.

She said, 'The man who wrote *Adventuring*, Michael...his name is Chuck Lane.'

Michael agreed, 'Yes. Yes, so it is. But...'

'I'm Chuck Lane.'

Michael didn't seem to understand. He still waited expectantly.

'Chuck Lane,' she repeated hopelessly.

Michael blinked, stared, studied her with such astonishment that she wondered, if in addition to her other troubles, something strange had happened to her face. At last he said, 'You? You wrote those books? You're Chuck Lane? Kay, are you sure that you...'

'That's me,' she said. 'And that's why I'm here. I need help. There are complications.'

But he wasn't yet ready for that. He spent more time simply sitting there, staring at her and chuckling, than Kay considered necessary. But finally, pulling himself together, he mused, 'They said all along you were up to something. But who would have believed...Sandra of course said it was some big affair that you didn't want noised around. Maybe with a married man...and all the time.' Michael stopped suddenly. Then, 'Now, Kay, really. Tell me the whole truth. I am your lawyer after all. Who helped you? Who did those scenes? You know, the big ones where...'

'Nobody.' Her icy tone indicated her displeasure. 'I don't need any help.'

Michael mused further. 'Up to something. That's what they all said.'

'I don't have time. It's either write or do it. But not both.'

He seemed dubious, but let it go to suggest that he and Kay, adjourn their meeting to a nearby bar where, they could, in comfort and conviviality, continue their discussions.

If he had announced his intentions, he could not have made them more plain.

Comfort, conviviality, sweet talk, a hand on a knee...and later, another adjournment for more comfort.

Kay said coolly, but with no amusement, 'Michael, I think I'll wait to discuss my problems with Mr Aker after all.'

Michael became all business. He sat back, the eager leer gone from his face. He shoved *Adventuring* into a drawer, and pulled a yellow legal-size tablet into position before him. 'All right,' he said briskly, 'now let's see what Aker and Devlin can do for you.'

CHAPTER 10

The Teachers

Kay had listened to a careful and detailed description, but not for the first time, of the first grade. She had, also not for the first time, exclaimed, explained, encouraged. She had made sounds of awe, sounds of commiseration. At last convinced that she was sufficiently impressed, Donnie collapsed into bed and to sleep with no bridge between.

She was on her way to the kitchen when the phone rang. It was Sam Golden. He said, 'Kay? How are you, Kay? It's been such a long time, hasn't it?'

It didn't seem long to her. She made a noncommital sound.

He took that for vigorous agreement. 'I thought, it you're not busy, I'd drop by.'

She reminded herself that she had known it would take Sam a while to figure out what her 'Goodbye, Sam' meant. She told him she was busy.

He said he saw. She hoped he did.

He obviously didn't. He went on, 'Amanda, that is your mother, she says...'

Kay had learned that she mustn't say the house was on fire. She thought bitterly of Jonathan Williams He should have known that wild comment to be just a manner of speaking. She suspected he had known it, but set out to teach her a lesson.

Sam demanded loudly, 'Kay, are you there?'

'Of course,' she said sweetly. 'Naturally. You called me here, didn't you? And I answered here, didn't I?' She wondered why she had been thinking of Jonathan Williams.

A moment of silence. Then, 'Never mind what your mother says. I've been thinking about the committee, Kay. Have you called a meeting yet?'

'No, I haven't, Sam.'

'School has begun.'

'Right.' Cheerfully.

'There'll be a P.T.A meeting soon.'

'I guess so.' Less cheerfully.

'Your committee should have a report.'

'I suppose so, Sam.' With no cheer at all.

'So it's time to get busy.'

Inspiration struck. 'Oh, Sam, sorry. Somebody's at the door.' She hung up. Once again she started for the kitchen.

Since her talk with Michael that morning, she had felt pure of heart and light of head. She had been assured and reassured that Chuck Lane would not bring disaster upon her. She was ready to take up *Bored, Chapter 6.*

There was a quick knock. The door flew open. Sandra cried, 'Kay, you there?'

Kay rocked to a halt. 'I'm here.'

Sandra surveyed the hall, the living room beyond. Kay herself. 'I thought I'd drop in for a minute. Want to run out to the club?'

'Not tonight, Sandra.'

Sandra sailed past Kay and wilted willowlike into the sofa. 'Michael's out on the town. Or somewhere. Or something.'

Kay resisted the impulse to play hostess. She resolved that she would not offer a drink, or coffee, or even conversation. She did allow herself to be pressed by Sandra's narrowed glance, into taking a seat, but perched there, as if ready to take wing at any moment.

'You certainly were out of it at the Thespians. I'll bet you don't even know what costume you signed up to do,' Sandra told her.

Kay thought. Blankness. She admitted it.

Sandra told her.

Kay wailed, 'Margery's? But that's the worst fitting job!'

Sandra smiled. 'See? I knew you were worried about something. Everybody could tell. I guess it was Margery and Ralph. I do feel...well, she is your sister, of course, but really, why should she, when she has Dick...and you and Ralph...'

Kay shuddered.

Sandra narrowed long dark eyes. 'I'll be darned if I'd let anybody, even my own sister, steal a man from me.'

'He is an...an oaf!'

Sandra appeared amused, and sympathetic. 'That's how it often starts.'

'What?'

'Love. First you think he's an oaf. Then you fall in love with him.' Sandra became reflective, a pose that hardly suited her, according to Kay. 'Yes. Maybe you have to hate those you love.'

'It seems improbable.' Kay knew that by being trapped into such a discussion, she was prolonging Sandra's visit. She sought a better subject, and immediately found it. Sandra loathed housekeeping. She felt the womanly arts beneath her. Kay said brightly, 'I've found the most marvellous recipe for banana cake. I'm going to bake some tonight. Come and watch me.' She rose. 'You take milk and add vinegar, and that gives you sour milk...'

Sandra had risen, too. 'Well, if you won't come to the club with me...' She moved quickly toward the door. 'Happy baking, dear!' and was gone.

Kay locked up. She went into the kitchen.

Accoutrements in proper place, she placed herself. *Bored, Chapter 6.* Into the sweet silence came a sound. She ignored it. It continued until she could ignore it no longer. She rose. The sound was a pounding at the door. Swearing, she unlocked it, opened it.

Ralph Parlmeyer stood there. He cried crisply, 'Kay! An impulse! I had to see you.'

He was plainly, to hear him, afloat on

a tide of uncountable Martinis.

She got her foot ready, but was too late.

He lurched by her, staggered down the hall, collapsed into the sofa cushions still dented by Sandra's willowy curves.

'I couldn't stay away,' he told Kay.

'You couldn't?'

'Seeing you last night brought it all back...'

'Ralph,' she sighed. 'Would you like coffee?'

'Coffee?'

'That's all I have.'

'If that's the best...'

She escaped into the kitchen. The percolator was blessedly there, ready, hot. She rattled and banged cups, loaded a tray, hurried back.

He was on his feet again, wavering, but on them. He stared at the tray she held. 'What's that?'

'Coffee.'

He came to meet her, disconcerting her by his sudden enthusiasm.

She didn't understand until he took the tray from her, put it carefully, but with cups, and sugar bowl dancing, on a table, and then swung back to her. She didn't really understand then. Not until he seized her, softly moaned her name.

He seized her. One big hand curled caressingly at her breast. Another big hand curled possessively at her bottom. She was pulled in hard, snugly, invitingly.

She considered that they were adequately aligned, anatomically speaking. But he made a few more quick adjusting movements while his mouth settled, sucking, on hers, and then slipped, tongue stroking, to nip her throat.

Enveloped, adjusted, stroked, nipped, caressed. It was all as it was supposed to be. But there was nothing *there*.

Kay pulled free, drew herself up. 'Really, Ralph...'

He reached, she ducked.

It took a little while, but at last he was gone, still staggering, still aglow, but with somewhat less enthusiasm.

She decided to sit down, to rest, to have a cup of coffee. It would clear her mind. It would settle her. It would.

A car pulled up outside. She waited.

Footsteps on the walk. She waited.

A gentle tap at the door. She answered it.

Michael grinned at her. 'I want to talk

to our famous author.'

She winced, said, 'Remember ethics, please. That's our secret, and not to be talked about, and...'

'Sure is our secret.' Then, 'Aren't you going to ask me in?'

'But what for?'

'So we can talk.'

'About what?'

'I still have some questions to ask you, Kay. I mean...it's pretty complicated stuff. I've thought about it. We're going to have to have several consultations.'

'You have an office, Michael.'

'Sure. Okay. Of course. But since I'm here...'

She knew better, but short of throwing him bodily through the door, she couldn't think of any way to keep him out. Particularly since he was in, and past her, and settled on the same rumpled cushions so recently occupied first by Sandra and then by Ralph.

Michael sat and beamed at her, blue eyes as unsmiling as always, and slightly reddened. His urbane manner was roughened at its edges. Obviously Sandra had been right. Michael had been out somewhere, doing something, that included taking large quantities of what might have been Martinis, bourbon, Scotch or vodka. Anyway, large quantities of something.

Kay poured two cups of coffee. She gave him one, which he accepted, and promptly put down without drinking.

Kay asked, 'What questions did you have in mind?'

'Well,' and he regarded her with a leer, 'now tell me, just tell me the truth, between you and me, and honestly, tell me where you get your ideas?'

'What's that got to do with...'

He was suddenly all sly dignity. 'After all, I'm a grown man. Take a good look at me. I'm a grown man, am I not? You don't suppose that I can't guess what you've been up to. Of course I can. So...'

She saw what the 'so...' meant. He was available. He was ready, willing, and considered himself able.

He confirmed that almost at once, still leering, 'Now you and I, between us, with the things I could teach you, the experience I could give you...between us, Kay, honey, you could really write a book!'

'Thanks,' she said dryly. 'I'm doing okay.'

'I've always had a letch for you.'

'Drink your coffee, Michael.'

'I know you've been around. Say, those things you write, honey. But what about me...'

'Drink your coffee,' she repeated, 'and then please take your letch some place else.'

'Or...say...listen, honey, tell me the truth. Are you one of those?'

'Those?'

He mused, 'You hardly go around with men. Everybody thinks you've got a man but you haven't.' His unsmiling, slightly red, blue eyes narrowed. 'Are you a les? Is that what's wrong with you?'

'Drink your coffee,' she said, and that was the third time.

Remarkably, either her words, or his, took effect. He reached for his cup, sipped, choked, stared at her. 'Sure. Sure. That's it,' he said thoughtfully. 'Or...' and his eyes brightened, his smile widened, 'say...no. You're not a les. But you're still in love with Earl!'

She stared at Michael.

He stared at her.

'Of course. You're still in love with Earl. After all this time. After the way he treated you. That is, the way I suppose he treated

200

you. My sainted father-in-law, old man Aker, has a mouth like a trap. Nothing comes out, nothing, ever, so I don't know the details, but...'

'An excellent quality for a lawyer,' Kay observed.

Michael finished his coffee, rose. 'We all have it.' Then, as if the pass he had made was her fault, 'You should have told me, explained. I would have understood.'

'What?'

'About you and Earl.'

She didn't answer.

'So obvious. *The Hot Stars, Loving, Adventuring.* I don't know why I didn't see it before.'

'What?' she repeated then.

'The way all your heroes are named Earl.'

It was a jolt that shook her to her very toes. She had known all along that she always used Earl's name. But she had never thought about it, never counted, never considered. Now, faced with it, she said thoughtfully, 'It must have been my way of reminding myself to watch out for great lovers.'

Michael grinned, ambled toward the door. He was obviously sobered. He was also obviously satisfied. She had rejected him, but his vanity was intact. He said, with masculine smugness, 'Whatever you say, Mrs Freud. Let's leave it at that.'

Kay was glad to. She saw him off. She locked the door behind him. She turned off all the lights, and stumbled into the kitchen.

CHAPTER 11

Return Of The Crusader

It was, Kay decided, strictly her own fault.

If she hadn't wanted any discussion about it, if she hadn't wanted to call attention to it, if she hadn't enjoyed her periodic glimpses of it, she would certainly have put away the stack of Chuck Lane's books with which Jonathan Williams had so thoughtfully provided her. She would have put the stack away in some sensible and secret place, such as the basement. It would have melted into the other stacks there, the author's copies, the final carbons.

It would have passed unnoticed among Donnie's outgrown crib, and the unused canning jars. But she *had* enjoyed those periodic glimpses of her books, and she had left them there, in clear sight, on the living room table. And with every enjoyable glimpse, she had thought of Jonathan Williams, and enjoyed that, too. Now it seemed to her suddenly that she had spent a substantial amount of time since their last meeting, looking at her books, and thinking of him.

That, of course, was ridiculous. She had too much on her mind to concern herself with him. Such as *Bored, Chapter 12.* Such as Galen's frequent letters of query. Such as how to spend a small portion of the second advance on *Doing It* without telling any more lies, or at the least, without getting caught at it. There was also the matter of Margery's costume for the Thespians' production. And...

And at the same time, Amanda, nestling within the soft satiny folds of her new ranch mink jacket, drifted in slow, model-like steps, first here, then there, and paused to pose, and in one of those pauses, reached out a slim, well-manicured and well-creamed hand to tap *Adventuring,* and said, 'My goodness, sweetheart, I hadn't realized...'

'Realized what?' Kay asked, and saw the tapping fingernail obliterate the Chuck Lane by-line.

'That you read such things as these. You'd be better off living them.'

Kay thought of Sam, Ralph, Michael. She thought of that interminable evening two weeks before.

'Living instead of reading. You can't possibly get anything out of reading that you wouldn't get out of life itself, only more so.'

Kay decided she definitely got more out of writing those books than she would out of living them. Aloud she said, 'Some women are maybe men oriented, and some are maybe not.'

Amanda stroked her mink jacket. 'Men aren't so bad.'

Kay thought that Amanda might more properly be saying that Sweet Cynthia wasn't so bad. Sweet Cynthia and her broadtail coat, size forty-four bust, and her Tuesdays and Thursdays. It was she who ought to be thanked, rather than James, for Amanda's new mink jacket.

'I ought to run,' Amanda said. 'I'm

meeting Carl, you know Carl Hessler, for lunch at the club.' Still posing, her delicately-shaped nose raised high, she drifted toward the door. She paused there, for the phone rang.

Kay answered it, conscious of Amanda's unashamedly listening ears, said, 'Oh, Sam. How are you?' and went on, repeating, for Amanda's benefit, each of Sam's remarks.

Thus: 'Oh, you're pretty good. So am I, Sam.' Then, 'Oh, for lunch? No. I can't. Amanda's visiting.' From behind her, Kay heard Amanda's whispered expostulation but ignored it. 'Another time? Thank you, Sam.' Then, 'The committee? No. I haven't. It takes some thinking over. Why did I miss the P.T.A meeting? I didn't have time, Sam. I was elected chairwoman? It would be good for me? That depends, Sam. How nice for Mrs Planter to be so active. I certainly did hear about the run on those books. Thanks for calling. Goodbye, Sam.'

Amanda hugged her mink jacket around her. It was, of course, much too warm for mid-October Indian summer. That would not deter Amanda, however. So, hugging the jacket around her, frowning, she demanded. 'Why did you do that?'

'What?'

'Treat Sam Golden that way!'

'I don't like his sons.'

'Ridiculous.'

Amanda sighed. 'It's true then.'

'What?'

'Sandra says you're withdrawing into yourself. And away from men. That you're turning into a...'

Kay groaned silently. Shades of Michael Devlin! She said, 'You better start collecting the butterfly nets.'

'It's no joking matter. Women who have been hurt deeply have been known to break. You only think you're immune, but...'

Kay thought of Jonathan Williams. That was *too* much. She wildly sought diversion, and found it. 'Amanda,' she said evenly, 'you are going to be late.'

Amanda glanced at her watch. 'I'm afraid I am. But I'm your mother, sweetheart. You don't know how a mother feels.'

'I'm one, too.'

It was Amanda's turn to ask, 'What?'

'I'm a mother, too. Remember? There's Donnie.'

'That's different. When children are little, a mother's worries are small. When children grow up, the worries grow with them.' Amanda presented the bromide as if it were freshly-minted coin.

Kay, having heard it a few times before in her life, recited it with Amanda, but silently. And when they both came to the end of it, Kay grinned, said, 'Don't spoil your day worrying about me.'

Amanda said with sad dignity, 'But I do,' and gasped, 'Carl's probably having a fit,' and opened the door. She opened the door and went into an odd little bob and weave. Sad dignity fallen, the silken mink tumbled around her slender ankles, she cried, 'What's the matter with you!'

Jonathan, hand upraised, fell back, his lean face suddenly touched with the delicate pink of early sunrise. 'I was just...' His hand dropped. In falling it just missed Amanda's aggressively tilted jaw.

'Assaulting a perfect stranger! Me!' Not only was her jaw aggressively tilted, but so was her silver-blond head. And her eyes were raised upwards, staring at him, and as she went on, her voice softened, asking, 'Or are we strangers?'

Lean face the flaming carmine of sunset, Jonathan swooped low and gathered silken mink. 'I was just...I am very sorry...please accept my...'

Pity overwhelmed Kay. She made hasty introductions. She said she was certain that Jonathan had been about to knock at the door, and that Amanda, opening when she had—

'Jonathan Williams?' Amanda trilled. 'Oh, you're the editor of the *Greenhill Sentinel*. My goodness, how very nice to meet you at last. The very best little newspaper I've ever seen. Why, yes. I always read it with a great deal of interest.' Out of breath, she paused.

'Your date, Mother?' Kate suggested, intrigued but not quite as intrigued as she ought to have been by this example of Amanda's technique.

'Date?' Amanda was suddenly vague. And to Jonathan, 'Do come in. You must let me apologize. I can't imagine what I was thinking...' She presented a slim shoulder to Jonathan. He gravely draped the mink jacket on it. She backed, filed, and drifted into the living room, to settle, a queen in regal robes, at one end of the sofa.

Jonathan grinned at Kay. 'How are the fires these days?'

'Burning,' she retorted.

Amanda patted the sofa near her. 'Do sit down, Jonathan.' Then, archly, 'Oh, forgive me. I may call you that? After all, the prerogatives of age.'

'Age?' He sat beside her. 'Why, when I saw you at the door, I thought, I thought you must surely be Kay's sister.' He turned to Kay. 'You don't mind if I call you that?'

'Kay's sister Margery?' Amanda asked icily.

It was plain that she did not appreciate the compliment. It was equally plain that Jonathan caught on quickly. He said, 'Or Kay herself.'

Mollified, Amanda informed him that he could certainly call Kay by her first name. They were, after all, all friends there, and...

Kay discovered that what was burning was burning very well indeed. A slow hot fire of anger, all-consuming, and surprising, seemed to be charring her within and without. Simmer in the blood, embers in the eye, prickles in the skin. She reminded herself that cool amusement was her strength and stand-by, her staff and rod.

She said through gritted teeth, 'Yes. We're all friends here,' and wondered what the all-consuming anger was about. She ought to be delighted that Amanda, unable to resist a good-looking, young, male face, had resettled herself, intending to see Jonathan's visit through from beginning to end.

'Your daughter,' Jonathan said, 'is certainly opposed to publicity.'

'Oh?' Amanda trilled.

'Wouldn't give me any details about the contests she'd won. And I've checked and I must say, I can't find a trace of...'

Kay said desperately, 'Would anybody like coffee? A sandwich? It's lunchtime.'

Amanda cut in, 'It's early, sweetheart,' and to Jonathan, 'She's so modest. I'll be glad to give you the details myself. We mustn't let her hide her light...' Amanda frowned faintly, 'Now let's see...it was a month ago...the car...' She turned to Kay, 'A month or longer? And what *was* that contest, sweetheart?'

More desperately, Kay said, 'You must be starving. I'll just fix you...'

Jonathan rose. 'But that's why I dropped by. I thought...well, how about it? Have lunch with me, Kay.'

'Don't you work?' Kay asked.

'I am working.'

'You are?'

His deep, drawling voice turned silky. His hazel eyes glinted. 'I wanted to talk to you about the committee, Kay. I figured that by now you've read the books I've brought you. I was hoping we could...'

'Of course you can.' Amanda drew her mink around her. 'Now the country club has a lovely lounge, and we can...'

'You take it off taxes? Expenses and all that?' Kay asked grimly.

Jonathan gave her a half-checked nod. 'Well, I can. But in this case, actually...'

'Sorry,' Kay said. 'I'm busy.'

'Kay, dear,' Amanda wailed.

'It's very important,' Jonathan said earnestly.

'Lunch at the club?' Kay demanded.

'No. Of course not. The committee. I mean...listen, don't you see? You can make Greenhill a laughing stock. And that Mrs Planter, she's going around...'

'You must listen, Kay,' Amanda urged.

'It's utterly ridiculous,' Kay sputtered.

Amanda and Jonathan stared at her.

'I mean...the whole thing.'

'The committee?' Jonathan asked quickly.

211

And at the same time, Amanda asked heatedly, 'Lunch at the club?'

Kay regarded them both, filled with despair.

Time. Time. Time.

And there the two of them sat, talking at her, talking at her while her arms prickled and her legs felt weak and she kept noticing, without wanting to, that Jonathan's shirt still missed a vital button, talking at her while time fled by, and bits and pieces of *Bored* wriggled in her mind like eels in a can.

'But have you read Chuck Lane's books yet? Can you honestly say, if you have, that they are dangerous? Can you honestly say that they are not honest?'

'I've read them,' Kay admitted weakly.

'Then?' Jonathan was triumphant.

'Then?' Amanda was with him.

'I do not care to discuss...'

'Kay, freedom of the press is one of the foundation stones of American life.' Jonathan's hands went to his russet hair. A quick nervous massage created crests of curls. 'The press,' he went on, 'definitely includes paperbacks.'

Amanda trilled. 'Are you in favour of...'

'Show me one girl ever ruined by a

book,' he demanded heatedly.

'You're quoting somebody,' Kay told him.

He agreed, admitted that he couldn't remember who.

She grinned.

He grinned back. 'Anyhow, we can talk about it, can't we?'

Kay was about to agree that they could at least talk about it.

But Amanda cried, 'Oh, I'm absolutely starving.' She swept her coat around her, regally rose. 'If this child of mine refuses the pleasure of your company at lunch, Jonathan, that is her affair entirely. I do not refuse. I accept the invitation. We can certainly talk about it over a nice chilled Martini, and a shrimp salad.'

Jonathan raised a dark brow at Kay.

She ignored it.

He rose, a repressed shrug implicit in the set of his shoulders. He said kindly, 'I wish I could make you see. I wish you'd give me a chance to show you how dangerous a thing your committee can be, Kay.'

The danger that confronted Kay at that moment, the danger that concerned her then, was that she would be charred, consumed, and returned to the elements of which she was made, by the fires that raged within her.

Amanda, blithely inviting herself to lunch with Jonathan...

He, supinely permitting himself to be manoeuvred...

He, allowing himself the luxury which no decent newspaperman could allow himself, the luxury of taking for granted, without checking...

Jonathan offered Amanda his arm. 'Shall we go then?'

CHAPTER 12

Several Moments Of Truth

At last there was sweet sweet silence.

Except that the refrigerator clicked on and off, and golden leaves rustled at the window, and crumpled sheets of yellow paper whispered along the linoleum.

Kay sighed, anxious fingertips hovering over the portable's tempting keys.

Starrleigh awoke in Earl's arms. Starrleigh awoke in Earls' arms. StarrleighawokeinEarl's arms. Starrleigh...

Kay sighed again. Time. Time. Time.

What was happening to *Bored.* To Chuck Lane?

At last there was sweet sweet silence, and, instead of *his* inspiration, Kay's own thoughts. They formed a steel screen between her anxious fingertips and the portable. They elbowed Chuck Lane out of the bright yellow kitchen, out of the house.

It had suddenly become insupportable that Sam Golden dared to nominate her to the committee to see about *those* books. (What right had Jonathan Williams to question her about what she did, about her beliefs?) It had suddenly become insupportable that she had allowed herself to be elected to that committee, that she had been faint-hearted and weak-minded. (What right had Jonathan Williams to lecture her?) It had suddenly become insupportable that she had not thoroughly and completely squelched that ridiculous committee the moment the matter had come up at the P.T.A meeting. (Who did Jonathan Williams think he was anyway?)

Her anxious fingertips tore the yellow sheets from the portable. They fitted white paper, carbon, yellow paper together, and set them, and went to work, hammering, punishing, sure. She wrote:

The Parent and Teachers Association
Greenhill Elementary School
Greenhill So and So
Dear Fellow Parents:
I hereby submit my resignation from the chairmanship of the committee set up to study certain types of books, as discussed at the first meeting of the year, the all-grade meeting. I also submit my resignation from the Greenhill Unit of the P.T.A. I do not wish to be a part of a committee, nor an organization which set itself up as watchdog over the reading habits of Americans. I do not believe in that kind of censorship. I do not consider myself, or anyone I know in this community to be qualified to act as such watchdogs.

Sincerely,
Chuck Lane

She reread the letter, her satisfaction just as intense as if she were rereading a newly-finished chapter. She smiled, sighed, and sealed it into an addressed envelope.

Holding the licked stamp poised, she stopped, frowned. Something bothered her.

216

She opened the envelope, reread the letter once more. Yes. Yes. It was all right. It was perfect, in fact. Just what she wanted to say. Then the signature hit her!

She swore. She typed again. That time the signature came out black, sharp, and her own. She affixed stamp, resealed the envelope. She rose, humming a martial tune, and to that martial tune she went out to the mail box.

Then home again, and once more sweet sweet silence. Except for the click on click off of the refrigerator, except for golden leaves whispering at the window, and crumpled sheets of yellow paper rustling on the linoleum.

Her anxious fingertips hovered over the portable's tempting keys. Tempting, but stubborn keys.

Starrleigh awakened in Earl's arms, and...
Kay sighed again. Now what?

In a little while, she began again. *Starrleigh awakened in Earl's arms. And* went on. *The room was filled with sunlight. She sat up and stretched, enjoying the sensations of her replete body, the love bruises on her thighs, the kiss bruises on her lips, the ache in her nipples. She slipped carefully from bed, hoping to allow Earl a few moments more of rest. But as she walked across the room, she felt his glance on her nude body. It was as close, as intimate, as stirring, as the touch of his hands had been a little while before. She felt herself respond to it with a quickening in her blood and a lift in her pulses. She drew herself up, walking tall and slim and straight, and, at the bathroom door, she paused, turned sideways to give him a profile of her small jutting breasts. Small jutting breasts small jutting breasts small...*

Kay sighed again. Now what?

Now what indeed.

It was definitely time for Amanda to stop looking like anybody's sister, and start looking like a mother. (What right had Jonathan Williams to take Amanda to lunch?)

She enforced rigid discipline. She brought her anxious hands down to the key board. She flexed her fingers. They wrote: *Earl's hand made curls of his russet hair. His hazel eyes glinted. He asked, in his deep drawling voice, 'Starrleigh, tell me. Why are you so afraid of love?'*

Kay paused to make a quick pencil scrawl on a paper scrap. It reminded her that Earl, in the middle of *Chapter 12*, had changed hair colour, voice, and character.

Then, smiling happily, she went on.

Sweet sweet silence gone into the machine-gun chatter of a bouncing typewriter...

Bored by Chuck Lane, Chapter 12. Chapter 13.

And suddenly a long time later, Donnie cried, 'Mom, I'm home. Can I have a peanut butter sandwich? And what does prim mean, anyhow?'

Kay allowed the peanut butter sandwich, defined prim in too many words.

Donnie licked his chin, chewed, and considered. Then, 'But what does it have to do with cars?'

'Cars?'

'Rick's mother...that's what she said. On the phone. I heard her. She always thought you were prim. Prim? Right? Only she guessed you weren't. There was such a lot of traffic around here lately.'

Kay bit off a thread studied the seam.

Margery's costume...cut to size, and that not easy since Margery was definitely gaining weight. Basted together now. Not bad. But Kay hoped it would hold until the next fitting, and hoped it wouldn't have to be enlarged, and hoped—

Donnie asked, 'What do you think I

ought to be on Halloween?' and put his feet up on the sofa.

Kay noticed, but said nothing.

'Halloween?' James Mason asked, and sipped his Scotch and soda. 'Halloween, Donnie? It's still weeks away.'

Like daughter, like father, Kay thought. The two of them fighting off time. And losing. Of course they were both losing. Kay raised her eyes to look at James. Yes. His temples definitely were more white, more distinguished-looking, that is to say. And she...well, never mind her temples. The stack of yellow paper was growing...*Chapter 17.*

Donnie was making horrible sounds, sounds which Kay adjudged to be sardonic laughter.

Finally, he controlled them. 'Halloween's not weeks away. It's tomorrow.' And, answering himself, 'Should I maybe be a cowboy?' And, answering himself further, 'Nope. Big hats are old hat.'

'Space man?' Kay suggested.

'Nope. Old hat, too.'

'Clown?' James offered, smiling an indulgent grandfather's smile for a change.

Donnie made a sour, stubborn, definitely Earl face.

Kay looked away.

James pursued what Kay ignored. 'What's wrong with being a clown?'

'Face make-up. Ugh!'

'All boy,' James said proudly, forgetting his predilection for girls.

'A ghost! That's what I'll be.'

'Good.' James approved. 'Fine. I'll take you out now, buy it for you.'

Kay wondered what was once again causing her father's sense of guilt. First the casual drop in, with the important look. Then the offer to buy a ghost costume. Resignedly, she told herself that she would find out soon enough. It had, no doubt, to do with Sweet Cynthia.

Aloud, Kay said, 'We'll make ghost costumes. That's half the fun.'

'We'll make them and I shiver and pretend I'm scared and pretty soon I am.' Donnie rolled from the sofa to the floor, howling with maniacal laughter, and then scrambled to his feet, and raced outdoors.

James sighed. 'So much energy.'

'Don't you feel well?' Kay asked.

He looked decidedly fit, except perhaps for small signs of dissipation around the eyes. But they were certainly no worse than the small signs of dissipation around the real James Mason's eyes.

Her father looked startled. 'Me? I'm fine. Only...' He studied his glass, plainly decided the drink was too weak, or too short, or that he needed a diversion. He rose, asked, 'You don't mind if I help myself to a sweetener?'

'Go ahead.' Kay threaded her needle, knotted the thread, took two long basting stitches, and waited.

He added a full drink to what had already been in his glass, hesitated over an ice cube, decided on one, a small one, hesitated again over soda, shot a look at her, and decided on some, but also a small one, a very small one, she noted uneasily.

Settled again, he sighed. 'I wanted to talk to you.'

Now she would find out what was bothering him. What he had done for Sweet Cynthia on one of those Tuesdays or Thursdays, or what he had foolishly promised her, or what he was thinking of promising her.

'It is all over town,' he said.

'It is?' she repeated, surprised. He usually had an extremely philosophical attitude toward gossip. In fact, he rather enjoyed it, even when it was about himself. Besides, it being all over Greenhill was hardly anything new.

'Your letter to the P.T.A,' he explained sadly. 'You can't imagine how everyone is talking about it.'

She folded Margery's Thespian costume and set it neatly aside. What was to come would require total concentration.

Her intuition had apparently taken a holiday. That was bad enough. But her memory had done the same.

In the intervening two weeks she had put so many words down on paper, so many many words about a russet-haired Earl, that her resignation letter to the P.T.A, written the last time she had seen Jonathan Williams, boy editor, publisher, and crusader, had been completely obliterated. Obliterated, that is, in her mind, but not, apparently, in the minds of Greenhill.

James was saying sadly, 'You can't imagine, really, what a furor it's caused. I wish you'd explain it to me, Kay. I wish...'

'There's nothing to explain.' She was tranquil, amused. 'Sam Golden shoved me into that committee business in the first place. I never agreed with him. I think it's one of those harebrained, know-nothing, campaigns that's basically dishonest. I should have said so in the first place.'

'You were wiser in the first place than in the second, I fear. Your reputation...'

Still tranquil, still amused, she smoothed her reddish-gold bangs. She raised her dimpled, but very determined chin. 'My reputation? Do you know that I am considered *prim?* I am also considered sly enough to have a *secret* lover. The only problem is that it's secret.'

'And now you are being called a person that *likes,* yes, Kay, *likes* dirty books.'

She choked. She swallowed. She grinned. 'Greenhill is the world's centre of hypocrisy.'

'Hypocrisy?' James considered, sipped his drink, sighed. 'Well, I suppose so. On the other hand, that suggests that there is some shame, too, some memory of the moral code, some fealty to that code, which...'

'Fealty to that code which will become operative only when old age sets in, and hormones slow down, and...'

'You are bitter,' James said. 'I'm

afraid that Amanda's right. Something is definitely happening to you.'

'I suppose something is.'

'You see? I admit, dear, it *is* really all silly. But it *is* harmless. So why don't you just rescind your resignation? You can do it so gracefully. You've always had a way with words. Rescind your resignation, go ahead with the P.T.A, the committee. And then people won't be saying that you want to deprave the children.'

'Is that what they're saying? Really?'

James looked uncomfortable. He preferred pleasantries. Then the phone rang. He looked relieved. He was delighted with the diversion. As Kay went to answer it, he took the opportunity to refresh his drink, strongly, Kay noted, as she said, 'Hello!'

'Kay! Listen! I apologize. Mrs Planter has just been in. Complaining! Imagine that! Complaining! It took her two weeks to get up the steam. Two weeks to give me the biggest news of the year!'

There was no mistaking the deep, drawling voice, even though it was now edged with enthusiasm, but Kay cut in, 'And who is this?'

'I want to congratulate you! You're a dear and sensible girl! You're...' Enthusiasm died. Her comment had apparently gotten through at last. Jonathan Williams demanded, 'Is this Kay Barrenger?'

'This is Mrs Barrenger,' Kay informed him. 'And this is?'

Dead silence greeted her question. She was stuck with it. She repeated it.

The deep, drawling voice tried for pomposity. 'This is Jonathan Williams. I am the editor of the *Greenhill Sentinel*.'

She was happy, for no reason that she understood, that having tried for pompousness, and missed it, the deep, drawling voice was now coloured with suppressed laughter.

'Kay,' it went on. 'This is news. I just have to talk to you.' A pause. Then, 'Your mother said I could call you Kay. So...'

'My mother isn't qualified to drop the formalities for me.'

A second pause. Then, 'Mrs Barrenger, about your letter of resignation...I wrote an editorial about it a few minutes ago. I want you to hear it. Between us, if you'll give me an interview, we can put the cork in the whole crazy idea.'

Kay drew a deep breath. 'My resignation is not news. It is all over town. And I can't talk to you now, Jonathan.' She shot a look at her father. He was sitting straight up on the sofa, and if a man could be all ears, he was all ears. He was, in fact, more beagle than man, at that moment. She drew another deep breath. 'Sorry...you see...' she fished wildly for an excuse, found none, and to her own dismay, blurted, '...you see, the house is on fire!' and hung up.

James was on his feet, gulping his drink.

She told him, 'Not really.'

'I gather "not really," ' he retorted. 'But if I know that young man, and after all that Amanda has said about him, I ought to know him, then I'm off. Because he's on the way.'

'On the way? Here?'

'After telling him that extraordinary thing, what do you expect?' James headed for the door. 'When he gets here you might inform him that you've changed your mind. You are going to push the committee, after all. You are its chairwoman. You will protect our children. And give Greenhill its place in the sun.'

'When he gets here?' she wailed.

'But that's what you wanted, isn't it?'

She didn't have time to consider, to confirm, nor to deny.

James departed saying. 'And *I* am not going to quarrel with that young man about censorship, freedom of the press, or dirty books.'

As he drove off, a tan sedan drove on. It careened into the lane, jerked to a stop before Kay's house.

Jonathan leaped out and loped up the walk.

His russet hair stood on end. His tie was askew. His jacket flapped wildly.

He said, 'You think you're pretty funny, don't you?'

'That was a pretty dumb thing to do,' she said ruefully. 'I admit it. Dumb both times.'

'You're damn lucky you didn't get fire engines both times. Can you imagine what the charges would be if I'd...'

'I can imagine,' she said weakly, too conscious of the prickles that prickled along her arms, of a certain peculiar wateriness in her legs. And at the same time, too conscious of her jeans, her hair, her...

He took advantage of her tone. He patted her cheek. He walked, uninvited, into the house.

'Company?' he asked, looking at the

glass, emptied, of course that James had left behind.

'My father. He just left,' she said, and wondered why she had bothered to explain. And wondered even more when she found herself asking, 'Would you like a drink?'

'Sure. Always.' But he sounded absent-minded, rather than enthusiastic. And when she started to pour his drink, he went on, 'Oh, look, don't fuss. Just listen to this.' *This* was a sheaf of paper drawn from his inside jacket pocket.

This had been, she decided, nestling close to where his heart must be.

Hazel eyes focused on the page, lean face grew light with the joy of battle. Slowly, dramatically, he read, 'Who is Chuck Lane?'

Kay twitched, paled, made a soft sound of protest.

'Who is Chuck Lane?' Jonathan repeated. And then, 'Chuck Lane isn't important. But what is important is the freedom of every American to read Chuck Lane's books. *If he wants to. If he wants to.* Those are the relevant words. If he doesn't want to, then he doesn't have to.'

Kay had recovered. She cut in, 'If you are leading up to a discussion of the committee, and I'm pretty sure you are, and a discussion of my resignation from it, and I'm pretty sure of that, too, then I'd better save your time. I don't want to hear any more.'

'It's all about you.'

'That's what I was afraid of.'

'But...'

'I'm sorry, Jonathan. I'm not interested in causes. I have things to do. And so now, if you'll excuse me...'

The crusader's light slid from his face. He looked disappointed, disapproving. 'I don't understand you.'

'Sorry.'

'A little excitement via the *Greenhill Sentinel* wouldn't hurt anybody. This is an *issue*.'

'Greenhill has excitement enough.'

Hazel eyes swept her. 'It's intriguing.'

'Thank you,' she told him. 'And now...'

'Definitely. Yes. You are.' He added, 'In a peculiar way.'

'Thank you,' she repeated, but doubtfully.

He went on, 'There is, definitely, something peculiar about you.'

Sandra chose that moment to appear in the hallway. Willowy, scented, as beautiful as ever, she cried, 'That's what I've been saying all along! Kay, dear, you must introduce me to this very astute young man!'

CHAPTER 13

Certain Suspicions Confirmed

Donnie had been a busy, squealing ecstatic ghost on Halloween.

Margery had been a complaining, restless subject for two costume refittings.

Now, with three weeks gone by, Donnie's greying ghost hung limp and reproachful behind the kitchen door, and Margery's costume lay limp and unfinished on the dishwasher.

The air was full of turkey and sweet potatoes and brisk November bite.

Kay looked, but didn't see. She breathed but didn't scent. She lived but wasn't cold.

Starrleigh and russet-haired Earl played out their last love scene. *'You'll never ever leave me again,'* he whispered. *'We belonged together at the beginning. We belong together now.' Slowly, very slowly, he found the zipper at the back of her blue dress, and opened it. Slowly, very slowly, he unhooked the bra beneath. His hands spread sweet flame on her silken skin as he drew the concealing cloth away, and let it fall to the floor. Then, gently, very gently, his fingers cupped her small breasts, stroking delicately at rosebud nipples. For a moment, she was still, bound by invisible restraints. But then, with a small wordless cry, she threw herself against him, clung to him. He raised her into his arms and carried her to the bed. He planted a hundred small kisses on her body, a hundred small kisses that flowered into delicious shivers, that made her want him closer and closer, so that, when he moved over her, she raised up and her legs locked his hips...*

Kay watched and her fingers faithfully transcribed what she saw into words that marched sweetly across the page. She worked on and on. Then she tapped a delicate period. She double spaced. And then wrote, THE END.

She yawned, then she laughed.

She was too numb to be tired, but not too numb to be happy. There it was. THE END. *Bored by Chuck Lane.*

She looked at the stack of yellow sheets, and suddenly her euphoria drained away, ice cube in a bonfire. *Bored. By Chuck Lane* unfortunately required rewriting and final typing.

She calculated quickly. If she could type forty pages a night, if she didn't get stuck on the revisions...

There had already been two letters from Galen Maradick. He was understandably nervous lest that possible hardcover deal fall through if she took too long. She was just as nervous. There might even be other letters from him. She didn't know. She hadn't taken the time to go to Rosemont. She had worked, worked, worked.

There had been a couple of diversions.

One night Sam dropped in, unheralded and unstrung. That was the kindest construction she could put upon what had happened.

He had barely been inside the door, when, having barely greeted her, he said, 'I've read those books you think so much of. Those Chuck Lane books. So *that's* why you resigned from the committee! *That's* why you like his books. It's what you really want.' Having so unburdened himself, Sam seized her. He seized her literally, firmly, bruisingly. Unheralded, unstrung, and soon unzipped, he proceeded to tell her what he thought she wanted. The skirmish that followed was brief, painful to Sam, and embarrassing to Kay. But that time he knew what she meant when she said, 'Goodbye, Sam.'

Now she shrugged the memory away.

If she could type forty pages a night, if she didn't get stuck on the revisions...

There remained Margery's costume. The house, laundry, cooking. There remained Donnie, family, friends.

She shrugged away the memory of those, too.

If she could...

She did. Ten days later, she parked the emerald-green car in the Rosemont lot. She stepped out, ankle-deep in slush, the remains of the seasons' first snowfall. She shivered inside her cloth coat, and thought of fur, and hugged the neatly-wrapped package under her arm.

That package was soon in the hands of the postal system, and she was on her way out, having discussed the world situation, the weather, and the way time flew with the grinning clerk who insisted on calling her Mrs Lane.

On her way out, and in her hand, were three letters for Chuck Lane. Britanica Company, Inc., and Galen Maradick, too, had been busy, indeed, she thought. And there, three steps away, lingering in front of the hardware store window, peering from behind the limbs of Christmas evergreens, was a familiar form, a familiar face. A familiar face, now sheepish, now smiling with false surprise.

'Kay! Imagine running into you here!'

'Hello, Earl,' she said dryly, and promptly slipped the letters into her purse.

'How are you? How's Donnie? It's been such a long time.'

'We're both fine.' She gave him a coolly amused look. Then. 'And it hasn't been long enough.'

'Oh, hey, listen, I've thought about you. I have a lot.'

She turned away. She took an incautious step, and slipped and staggered. He steadied her.

'Real winter, Kay. You've got to watch yourself.'

Dignity intact, she agreed, thanked him, once again turned away.

He went with her. 'I've been thinking, Kay. I ought to see more of Donnie.'

'If you insist.'

'I do.'

'You have the legal right to. Although you've never overexercised it.'

'It's going to be different.'

She didn't like the sound of that. She wondered why it was going to be different.

'Could I come over now?'

'Now?'

'Why not? When you put things off, that's how time...'

'Donnie's not home from school until three o'clock. Don't come until then.' She slipped and sloshed away from Earl's protest.

Later, she told herself that she should have know better. After all, she had known *Earl* better.

He arrived moments after she did. Such a few moments after that the letters were still in her purse, unread, unhidden, and undestroyed.

A very few moments after *his* arrival, Sandra presented herself, all glossy, cooing surprise.

Kay knew instantly how it was that Earl just happened to be in the Rosemont

Shopping Centre, and knew instantly why he had a sudden yen to see Donnie.

It was just the sort of plotting which Chuck Lane would never permit himself. Too obvious. That's what Chuck Lane would say.

But Sandra and Earl were obvious. So...Sandra had been having an affair with Earl, but a Rosemont-based affair just wasn't enough. Nothing ever was for Sandra. So Earl had to meet with Kay, visit Donnie, meet Sandra all over again, and then...then...why Earl Barrenger would be Greenhill-based, and...

'So nice to see you again,' Sandra said, narrowing her long dark eyes. 'It has been ages, hasn't it? You haven't changed a bit, Earl.'

Earl's answer, 'Neither have you,' was more restrained, but the eager blue look he bestowed on Sandra was not.

Alas, Kay had once known Earl well. Too well. She instantly scented bourbon, bed sheets, and perfume.

She resolved to be patient, coolly amused, and totally hoodwinked, while she observed Sandra's machinations.

But Donnie, that dependable shrill-voiced diversion, arrived just in time.

In time because Kay's cool amusement charred at its edges very soon. And Earl, having made suitable gestures toward his bewildered son, soon rose to go. Once again he and Sandra exchanged glances.

Once again Kay scented bourbon, bed sheets, and perfume.

Sandra said, 'Since you're in the neighbourhood, Earl, why don't you have dinner with us? I know Michael would like to see you again.' And turning to Kay, 'And you, too, of course. After all, we're civilized people, aren't we?'

Earl accepted the invitation quickly, and left.

Kay demurred, but only briefly. She was too curious to allow herself to miss the next act of Sandra's little play.

Soon, allowing hardly enough time to create an impression of decency, Sandra, too, departed.

At last Kay was able to reach for her purse, and did. She dismissed smug, self-satisfied cat with creamy whiskers Sandra, and worst man in the world Earl, and studied the three letters from Britanica Company, Inc. They were all three the same, but each written with rising urgency. The last:

My dear Chuck:

How are you coming on the new one? It's taking too long. Hurry!! We don't want interest in your work to cool. Now—re requested biography—we still haven't received it. Maybe it was lost in the mail. Maybe you haven't yet sent it. Seriously, we need it. Seriously. A lot of young writers (you are young, aren't you? You must be, an old man couldn't remember enough to write like you) a lot of young writers have that independent attitude. Wrong. Wrong, Chuck. No man is an island (see the quote that Ernest took the title from). As your agent, I could do better for you if I knew you better. Anyhow, send bio. Or, if you're too busy, call me, Chuck. CALL me anyhow. Do that, will you?

Very warmest regards,
Galen.

So...

Kay sighed. Chuck Lane had no telephone voice, no biography. But he was definitely making a dent in her life. She grinned, got out the portable. The short note she wrote to Galen said only that the new book,

239

Bored, had been mailed that morning. She (that is, Chuck Lane, he) would be anxious for Galen's reactions. Period. End of note. Signed etc.

It was, Kay reminded herself as she dressed that evening, something of a celebration.

A secret celebration, to be sure. But *Bored* was done, and mailed. Credit due to an idea conceived at the last Devlin dinner that Kay had attended. Thus it was just that Kay should, once again, be having dinner there. And who knew what might occur to Chuck Lane then?

In honour of the occasion, she wore a v-cut velvet dress, the v exposing creamy curves of round high breasts, the long sleeves covering slender arms with graceful suggestiveness. She would, if challenged, pass it off as a little second-hand thing she had picked up in the nearly-new shop. It was, in fact, a sixty-dollar dress, brand-span new, and the sense of being swathed in velvet armour that it imported was worth every one of the sixty dollars it had cost her.

She daubed a last touch of Shalimar on her ears.

Lee Berg arrived. He took a look at her, a prolonged hungry look, then whistled a prolonged hungry whistle. 'Mrs Barrenger, you are...you are...by all the grey skies outside, you are cool!'

She assumed that was meant to be a compliment, and wondered when he had begun to notice that there were, after all, two sexes.

'Listen,' he said, still awed, but growing confidential, too, 'Maybe you can tell me what to do.'

She said cautiously, 'I could try, Lee.'

There was a knock at the door.

Lee grumbled, fell over his feet, but managed to get there, to open it.

Earl grinned at Kay, grinned and whistled, and, she thought, generally behaved like a junior version of Lee. The unwanted approval, delivered out of habit, she was certain, took a while. But finally he explained his presence. 'I figured you'd need a ride. And since I was passing...'

'I have a car,' she said.

'You do? Well, since I'm here...'

It would do Sandra good, if Kay in black velvet, and Earl, in panting condition, arrived together, Kay decided. And a few extra moments with the worst man in the world would hardly do Chuck Lane any harm, and might do him, Chuck Lane, some good.

Later Kay told herself that it did Chuck Lane a substantial amount of good.

Sandra's creamy whiskers looked not quite so creamy when Earl and Kay came in together. But Michael, sliding unsmiling blue eyes at Kay, laughed until he choked. Kay regretted that he did not.

Furthermore, as the evening progressed, with Sandra having repossessed Earl's attention, and observant Michael was seemingly blinded by Kay's black velvet, Kay, in a moment of utter boredom, laced with the insight of desperation, came up with the idea for plot and title of the next Chuck Lane book. *Society's Proprieties* was started some time between coffee and brandy.

And some time after coffee and brandy, in one of those silences broken only by Earl's heated breathing, and Sandra's purrs, Earl tried to distract himself and her, and maybe the rest of them, by reaching into his pocket and pulling out a copy of *Doing It.*

The warmth of the celebration, of

creation, and of brandy, immediately died out of Kay. She became a vulnerable icicle in black velvet. She thought herself unmasked, undone. She thought Earl surely knew and saw.

It was apparent that Michael thought the same. He was still, his face expressionless, watchful eyes studying Earl for that weakness which could be exploited in Kay's defence. There were weaknesses aplenty, but she knew of none that would save her.

But Earl grinned. 'Boy, I tell you, this is the book all right! Nobody should miss it. No wonder everybody's talking about this Chuck Lane.'

Kay relaxed. That is, she wilted in relief.

And with the relief came quick incredulous joy. *Doing It* was out, on the stands, being sold, read, talked about. *Doing It* was in print. And she hadn't even known it.

Earl went on. 'You ever hear of this guy? You read his stuff? I tell you, no wonder it's hard to get hold of. Hot. Real. True. A man's stuff.'

'Who did you say?' Kay asked.

'Chuck Lane.' Earl gave Kay a disgusted

and pitying look. 'Of course, you, being you, wouldn't...'

Michael said hastily, 'Everybody in Greenhill knows Chuck Lane. Knows about him, I mean.'

To Kay's relief, Sandra put on a group of records, held her arms out to Earl, and that took care of Chuck Lane. As far as the others were concerned.

But Kay spent the next hour on *Society's Proprieties*, unashamedly making mental notes on Earl, Sandra, and Michael. She was confident now that she was quite free to say anything about anybody. Nobody knew himself. The crackpot letter writers saw themselves in the strangers they wished they were. The real subjects saw themselves through *their* own eyes, too.

The way home:

Sudden snow softly falling, whispering tyres, whispering windshield wipers, and, regrettably, from Kay's point of view, whispering Earl.

He said, 'You look so wonderful tonight, Kay. It makes a man think.'

She thanked him coldly.

'All this time wasted.'

She advised him that she hadn't been

wasting her time. She had been extremely busy. And supposed that he had been busy, too.

Arrived:

She thanked him for the ride, polite, curt, and already reaching for the door.

He moved closer, took her hands. His arms came around her.

She remembered when Earl, and only Earl, could bring out the virago in her, could turn her from a sweet-tempered, quiet, tranquil soul into a shrill, raging fishwife. But, she reminded herself, she no longer cared. That made the difference.

She said coolly, 'Don't be ridiculous, Earl.'

His arms tightened. His mouth, half-smiling, tender, yearning, familiar, came down on hers. Then, 'Kay, I need you. I want you.'

She said, 'Why, Earl, you're...you're the living end.'

'Honey, come on...let's go in. Get comfortable.'

She went rigid on stiff, steely rage. 'You just can't...you find it impossible...you couldn't risk it, could you?'

The half-open tenderly-smiling, yearning mouth demanded, 'What's the use of talk?

You know what I want. And it's what you want, too. So let's...'

'You couldn't risk passing up a chance! Even *I* am a chance. That's what you're thinking! You're the same old Earl, all right. Put a woman, any woman, anywhere near you, and you've got to make her. You can't risk letting anything go by.'

One thing gone by was his yearning look. He snapped. 'Still picking on me, belittling me. Well, I ought to remind you, honey, *You* can't risk passing this chance with me by. You're all alone, aren't you? And have been for a long long time. And you sure got used to it, and liked it, and needed it. So you must be hurting. Hurting bad. I know you don't get many chances. And here I am...at least I'm your ex...and I know what you like, so what are you...'

A second thing gone by was the sweet-tempered tranquil quiet soul. Kay turned within the circle of his arms. She screamed, shrilled, 'I can sleep with anybody I want to, you oaf,' and slapped his face hard. Then she flung herself from the car, skidded through ankle-deep slush, wept into falling snow, and found herself inside.

Lee Berg called, 'That you, Mrs Barrenger?'

She couldn't play the usual dialogue game with him. She managed a choked, 'Yes. Yes, it's me, Lee. And you'd better go...'

She paused there. Tongue frozen, snow-flakes and tears on her cheeks, coat half on half off, she paused.

Lee appeared in the living room doorway. And looking over him, smiling a cordial welcome, was Jonathan Williams.

It was too much.

Kay didn't feel up to it.

She needed a breathing space.

But Jonathan said, 'I hope you don't mind, Kay.'

'We've been having the greatest conversation,' Lee told her.

'I was passing by...I just had the impulse...' Jonathan explained.

'He's a science fiction buff, too,' Lee said.

Jonathan's elbow moved.

Lee gulped. 'I guess I got to go.'

'Let's have some cocoa first,' Kay suggested sweetly.

Lee started to agree, his face all enthusiasm. He changed agreement to refusal, his face all regret.

Kay urged.

Jonathan's elbow moved again.

Lee departed sadly, an admiring look at Jonathan, a hopeless look at Kay.

When he was gone, Jonathan said, 'Come on in, Kay. Take your coat off. Have a seat. Or...say...the cocoa idea sounds great.'

'Thanks, Jonathan.' She put her coat away, turned to find him staring at her, an odd light in his eyes.

'That dress...it sure is...'

'Thanks, Jonathan,' she repeated.

'You look...not that you don't always...I've noted that you do...but somehow you look...'

'Nearly new shop,' she explained, thinking it odd that a newspaperman, an editor, a publisher, should have so much trouble expressing himself in words.

'Nearly new shop? I'll have to do a story on that. Thanks for the idea.'

'You're welcome. But remember not to mention my name.'

'Print-shy, aren't you?' Then, 'And that reminds me, the reason I dropped by...'

'Oh? Your impulse, you mean?'

'Impulse?' He seemed bewildered for a moment. Then his lean face cleared. 'Oh, yes. That. Well, you see, I've heard about your resignation from the committee, and from the P.T.A, and I wanted...'

She thought it odd that a newspaperman, an editor, a publisher should have so short a memory. She said gently, 'We've already discussed that at greater length than I cared to.' She summoned as much dignity as she could from her black velvet armour. 'There's no more to be said.'

'We've discussed it?'

'Certainly. You wrote an editorial. You wanted to read it to me!'

'Is that so?'

'Jonathan, do you have an amnesia problem? Yes. We discussed it. At least you gave me your ideas quite firmly. And furthermore, you might do me the courtesy of remembering it, since the resignation was really all your fault in the first place. I would never even have...'

He drew himself up. All six feet of him stiffened with indignation. '*My* fault?'

'You had already convinced me that the committee was ridiculous, so...'

'The committee? Sure. So you resigned from it! But the P.T.A. What about that? No. Absolutely no. You resigned from the P.T.A, and left those kooks, Sam Golden, Mrs Planter, a clear field. You should have stayed to fight them! I never say quit! I never say resign!'

'And I never fight.' She was, she thought, almost as brazen a liar as he was. Impulse had not led him to her house that night. And she had just given Earl a good fight.

Jonathan moved a step closer. 'You don't? Kay, really. You don't fight?'

She moved a step back, then a second step back. She had an idea that somehow, in some mysterious way, the subject had been changed.

The light in his hazel eyes had become an absolute glint. He moved closer again, very close indeed. He seemed very pleased.

'Why, Kay, you're just a scared, innocent little girl, aren't you?'

She thought of Earl. She looked at the three Chuck Lane books still joyfully placed where she could see them, and soon to be joined by *Doing It,* where she could see it too. She considered the germinating *Society's Proprieties.*

She said finally, 'Jonathan, I don't know how you ever guessed the truth about me. But you're right, of course. I'm just a scared little girl.'

'And I think I'd better go home,' Jonathan answered.

CHAPTER 14

Dangerous Success

'Mom!'

She ignored the first call.

'Mom!'

She tried to ignore the second.

'Mo-ther!'

She faced defeat, and sighed, and closed the quotation, banged a period into the wrong place, and then rose stiffly, to go to the bedroom.

Donnie reared up, aggrieved. 'I called you forever.'

'How come?'

'I can't sleep.'

'You wouldn't let yourself.'

'I tried. I can't. It's the reading, Mom. Why is THE the?'

Chuck Lane would hardly have an illiterate child. Kay Barrenger did. She explained why THE is the. She said, 'Because it is. Now go to sleep.'

Donnie leaned back and brought up big

guns. 'Why is Dad coming around now?'

That was a good question. It had gone on for too long. Having allowed it, out of curiosity, to involve her and Donnie, she had found herself unable to stop it. But she would not explain Earl to his son. Nor would she explain Sandra. There was time before he had to understand Greenhill's proprieties.

She said, 'Your father likes to see you.'

Donnie answered, 'That's not why, Mom.'

She was had, hooked, done in, out-fired. Donnie wasn't really worried about Earl's presence. Donnie had learned to take it, or leave it alone. And *it* was Earl. But, like every divorcee, Kay had moments of guilt, qualms, fears that in doing what she had to do for herself, for her self-respect, even her sanity, she had slighted her son. Even though she knew that she, and her silly guilt, was being exploited, she succumbed. She drew Donnie into her arms, rocked him, and held him, and lied firmly, 'Listen, Donnie, your Dad misses you. That's why he comes around,' and in the same comforting tone. 'What about some ice cream?'

They were tacticians out of the same

school. Just as his ploy had worked earlier, so her ploy worked now.

Donnie yawned over ice cream, fell asleep licking his lips.

She tiptoed back to the portable and to *Society's Proprieties.*

It was not easy going, though it should have been. She ought to have been able to put down the thinly-veiled story of Greenhill in her sleep.

But something had happened. *Bored,* fulfilling Galen's oft-repeated hope, had sold hardcover. It would be in the bookstores, fat, stacked, selling for six ninety-five.

And Kay was suddenly scared.

Now Galen Maradick and Britanica Company, Inc. jubilantly insisted that they had to have a picture of Chuck Lane. They had to have a biography. They had to meet with him, talk to him, to consider the possibilities of publicity, to...

Galen was jubilant, full of plans.

Kay was just plain scared.

She should have been able to put down *Society's Proprieties* in her sleep. But she was too scared, and too sleepy, to work.

She gave up and went to bed, and dreamed that she was walking nude, alone, in the hard brilliant sunlight of noon, through the Saturday crowds of suburbia in the Rosemont parking lot.

'Extraordinary,' Ralph said, putting a well-mannered hand on the four Chuck Lane books. 'You see them everywhere. A perfect example of contemporary values. Sex. Sex. Sex.'

Margery's pout turned to interest. 'Maybe I ought to read them.'

Kay took a final stitch, snapped the thread. 'All done,' she said brightly, and handed Margery the costume. 'You can iron it, can't you?'

'I suppose,' Margery agreed.

Ralph went on, 'I'd do a couple of them myself, if I had time.'

Kay suddenly realized that she had grown accustomed to his sober diction. She no longer translated to herself. She wondered how he would sound to her when he had tanked up on Martinis. Then she decided that she didn't really want to know.

He continued, 'All you need is a curvaceous blond heroine. Big breasts, white satin thighs. And a big big sexy hero...big...'

Kay cut in hastily, 'Anybody want coffee?'

Margery, her thoughts plainly elsewhere, sighed, 'Oh, yes.'

Ralph agreed. 'Sure.'

Dick Bellows shouted, 'Nobody move!' and charged the doorway, as if knocking invisible opponents aside. He was hatless and coatless. His clean-cut face was a hot flaming red. With him came the bitter cold of a mid-March night. With him also came the searing singeing heat of dead-end rage.

Margery cried, 'Now...Dick...now Dick... Dick...'

Ralph hastily took his hand from the cover of *Doing It*.

Kay asked plaintively, 'What's the matter, Dick?'

'Caught you in the act, you wife stealer!' Dick roared. 'You think I don't know what's been going on behind my back!'

Kay murmured, unheard, 'Costume fitting, Dick.'

He roared, 'Well, I do. And I won't have it. I ought to punch you in the nose!'

He apparently decided, hearing those words, that he not only ought to, but would.

He swung a wild roundhouse at Ralph's head.

Ralph went down hard.

The stack of Chuck Lane books went down with him.

Kay winced for the books.

Margery screamed, 'Dick, Dick, darling, did he hurt you?' and rushed into Dick's arms.

'No! He didn't hurt me!' His arms closed around her. 'And you stay away from him! I'm telling you, Margery, you just stay away from him, that's all.'

Margery sobbed, 'I didn't know I mattered to you anymore!'

Dick yelled, 'All right. You win. But goddam it, you better remember to take those pills.'

Kay murmured goodbye and godspeed to the backs of the happy, excited, and thoroughly-libidinous couple.

She put compresses on Ralph's swollen ear, and at last, he was on his feet, saying, 'I could write a book, Kay. Greenhill is ripe for it. Really, what goes on here...if you only knew,' and finally she murmured goodbye and godspeed to his departing back.

She salvaged the costume from the floor,

where Margery had dropped it when she rushed into Dick's arms.

She folded it and put it away for future delivery.

Sweet, sweet silence.

She headed for pantry and portable. At last, at last...

Amanda said, reaching for the cookie bin, 'I'm starved.'

Kay dropped a good China cup. It shattered. 'Oh? Want some raisin toast?'

'Raisin toast?' Amanda looked nauseated. 'I have a yen for Social Tea biscuits. Not raisin toast.' Once again she stretched for the cookie bin. 'But whatever you have...'

'No cookies. What about fruit?'

Amanda looked nauseated again. 'No fruit. Social Tea biscuits.'

'We'll get you some while we're shopping.'

'If I can wait.'

Kay attempted diversion. She said, 'I guess things are going to be better with Margery. I mean now that Dick...'

Amanda snorted. 'It's about time.' She shook her silver-blond curls. 'I don't know what the world is coming to. Men. Men. Men. That's all anybody thinks about these days.' She rose decisively, hugging her mink coat around her. 'Let's go now.'

Amanda's yen led them to the supermarket where they ran into Jonathan. While he greeted them enthusiastically, Amanda munched tea biscuits.

Kay noted with amusement, then alarm, that her mother finished the box, took another and started on that, ignoring Jonathan's presence, and his, 'Didn't I tell you, Kay? Golden and Mrs Planter are kooks. You can't imagine the problem. My problem. They are on me all the time.'

'So sorry,' she murmured, still eyeing Amanda.

Jonathan surged closer to her.

She felt prickles in her arms, a weakness in her legs, a strange warmth in her chest. She decided that she must be coming down with the end of March flu. She decided that she even felt a bit feverish.

Jonathan surged even closer.

She leaped back before she could stop herself.

He grinned. 'Remember our last conversation? See and take note.'

'I suffer from failing memory,' she told him coldly.

'If you had listened to my editorial...' he began.

She wandered away, leaving him in the middle of his sentence, and Amanda in the middle of her Social Tea biscuits.

Later, when Amanda caught up with her, she said, 'Kay, I want you to remarry. You must learn how to treat attractive young men!'

'But a little while ago, you told me...'

'That's different. Margery's married. Now I want you to be sensible. Jonathan is very nice.' She chewed vigorously. 'And he likes Social Tea biscuits, too.'

Kay decided that she had better go home.

Society's Proprieties

The usual lists, chores, distractions, filled the swift days of a swiftly passing month.

It was suddenly April's end, with sweet cool air full of promise, and budding forsythia and misty green in the trees.

With the manuscript on the seat beside her, Kay drove to Rosemont. She prayed silently but thoroughly over *Society's Proprieties*, and handed it to the clerk who said, with an admiring, springlike look at her legs, 'Good to see you again, Mrs Lane. Come back soon, Mrs Lane.'

She stopped at her box and found

two more letters from Britanica Company, Inc., Galen Maradick. She sighed. More impossible importunities, no doubt. As she flicked the box shut, a plump, freckled hand fell on her shoulder. A short, round man leaned close to her.

He said in a gravelly roar, 'Mrs Lane! I sure am glad to catch up with you at last! Your husband is one hard man to find!'

She had grown almost accustomed to being called Mrs Lane, but her *husband?* Husband? Momentarily, she was mercifully all at sea.

The short, round man leaned closer still, his freckled hand still on her shoulder tightening. 'You are Mrs Chuck Lane, aren't you?'

Sadly, being all at sea came to an end.

She knew that she was, must be, Mrs Chuck Lane. She coolly admitted to that identity. And, slightly less coolly, demanded, 'But who are you?'

'Ted Blake. That's the name.'

She regarded him bleakly. His eyes were warm brown, sharp. His half-bald head was tufted erratically with reddish fuzz. She drew her sweater around her.

'Ted Blake. But just call me Ted.' He grinned widely. 'I guess you're pretty surprised to see me all right.'

She agreed that she was.

'I'm a representative of Britanica Company. And Mrs Lane, you've just got to help me. This is really important. To you, to Chuck and to me. He has to consider the situation now. It's not like it was. His book, *Bored*, will be coming out in another five months. Yes. And in hardcover. Consider, Mrs Lane. There's publicity, the future possibilities...' Ted Blake's ruddy colouring seemed suddenly less ruddy. 'That is...I mean, now you stop and think about it, Mrs Lane. Your husband's books will be in the public eye, make news.'

'And his paperbacks?' she asked coldly.

'Oh, sure. People read them, too. But different. Hardcover readers know more and want to know more, and they care, and then the critics.' Ted Blake's gravelly voice grew weak. He seemed to wither under her stare. 'Well, it's like this, maybe I better tell you frankly. All of a sudden we, the company, I mean, we started thinking, they started, I mean. Look. Who knows? Maybe there's no Chuck Lane at all. After all, there's no Galen Maradick, so...'

'No Galen Maradick?' she demanded.

He confided in his gravelly whisper, 'No. None. It's just a name.'

Kay grinned. 'I did wonder.' Then, hastily, 'That is, we wondered.' And further, 'So what?'

'So what?' Ted shuddered. 'It's entirely different, that's so what. *Bored* in hardcover, and going great guns maybe. Big, big, big, Mrs Lane. Maybe it'll go to the movies. The movies even! And if it does, think of the position we're in. We don't know Chuck Lane from Adam. Maybe he is Adam. Suppose he's some kind of a nut? Suppose he's a plagiarizer? Suppose he is a libeller? Suppose...'

'As you said in the beginning, "Suppose he doesn't even exist?" Kay told Ted sweetly. She ignored his glum nod. She stepped out from under his freckled hand. 'Don't worry. I'm here to testify that there is a Chuck Lane. And he isn't a liar, or libeller, or plagiarist, or whatever it is that you're worried about. But there is one small thing I better tell you right now. He *is* a recluse. He is not available now, nor will he ever be. So the best thing for you to do is to go back to Brianica Company, and Galen...' She paused. Then, 'No. Never mind Galen. Just tell them not to worry, but to forget about seeing Chuck Lane.'

Ted looked hurt. 'Say, Mrs Lane, you don't even give me a chance to explain your self-interest.'

'I already know it.'

'Then tell me a couple of things to take back. I mean...all right. We won't bother you, or your husband. But suppose you tell me where you live.' He grinned winningly. 'I mean, surely not in that post office box.' She didn't smile, so he went on. 'Say you just give me an address. Maybe a phone number. One of these days maybe you can sneak a picture into the mail to us, and then...'

'Sorry.' She remained sweet, but firm. 'I couldn't. No. Impossible. And now, if you'll excuse me, Mr Blake.'

She didn't wait to find out if he would or did. She hurried outside, let sweet April air carry her to the car. As she pulled away, she saw Ted Blake climb into a cab.

Instead of taking the familiar highway to Greenhill, she drove into the city. She circled, stopped, circled, and finally, she parked the car. She had coffee in a drugstore. She checked a couple of bookstores. She window-shopped for half an hour, scanning every masculine form that approached or passed. She didn't see a short, round, red-tufted man.

Well-satisfied with herself, she drove back to Greenhill. As she pulled into the lane, Sandra's car spun past her with an angry grinding of angrily-abused gears. Kay smiled, delighted that she had missed Sandra's visit.

Moments later, she stopped smiling. When she got out of the car, she found Ted Blake waiting for her.

He gave her a hopeful apologetic smile. 'Listen, I'm sorry. Only it's what I get paid for. I've just got to see your husband.'

'If you don't stop bothering me...' she began, and stopped, and then, 'and what do you mean by following me anyway?'

'Follow you?' Ted's gravelly voice shook with shock. 'I wouldn't do that. Oh, no. I just happened to think, that's all, and I called the office. And I got them to check the queries for addresses. And there was a query all right. From here, Mrs Lane. Just that one thing. And after that, the P.O box, but I figured...what the hell, take a chance, so here I am. And here you are.'

She prepared herself to use any means necessary from seduction to assault, to get him away from the house. Prepared, but with no time in which to proceed. For Earl suddenly opened the door, and appeared on the front steps.

Ted whirled. He scurried up the walk, plump hand out-thrust, crying, 'Mr Lane! Chuck! I'm happy to meet you at last!'

CHAPTER 15

The Razor's Edge

'Mr Lane! Chuck! I am so happy to meet you at last!'

Ted Blake's gravelly voice seemed amplified by a giant size bull horn, a boom of hail-sized words. It seemed, to Kay, to drown Earl's irate shout, and Donnie's outraged cry.

Earl: 'What kind of a mother are you, anyway? Do you know what your son just said to Sandra?'

Donnie: 'Why were they messing around on my bed anyway!'

A boom, a shout, a cry!

Cross fire!

Kay flung herself into the fray, not bodily, but verbally. First, 'Mr Blake, I want you to meet Earl Barrenger. My *ex*-husband. And this is our son Donnie.' Then, 'Donnie, why don't you go see what Rick is doing?' And, 'Earl, why don't you...'

Ted Blake's red-tufted head was suddenly red all over. He let his out-thrust hand drop. He looked from Kay to Earl, and raised his hand again. He said, grabbing Earl's unwilling fingers, and squeezed them. 'Beg your pardon. Didn't know. A pleasure to meet you.'

It was impossible to know what Ted was thinking. Kay decided that she didn't want to know. She seized the social moment created by his attempt at tact, and said, 'Thanks for dropping in, Earl,' and, 'On your way, Donnie,' and, 'Please come inside, Mr Blake.'

The three males regarded her, open-mouthed and suddenly silent.

She turned her back on them, went briskly into the house.

She would not permit herself to think of the crossfire exchange which had greeted her. That would have to be dealt with later on. Now there was Ted Blake to attend to.

He, trailing her, did not look as if he wanted to be attended to. He turned suspicious brown eyes from here to there in silent search. Finally, no longer silent, he demanded, 'But where's Chuck?'

Tranquil, she took off her sweater and put it away. Tranquil, she smiled. 'Welcome to my house. Now wouldn't you like a drink?'

'But where's Chuck?' Pause, 'A drink? Say, that would be great.'

His instant enthusiasm cheered her. She danced away to the kitchen for ice cubes, and danced back. She mixed Scotch and soda and ice cubes in decidedly unequal proportions. She handed him the tall glass, hoping he wouldn't notice the colour of the drink.

He didn't. He drank deeply. His red-tufted head became redder still. His warm brown eyes, his suspicious brown eyes, gleamed. Then, 'Good. Good. Thanks. And now, now that I'm here, where *is* Chuck?' His gleaming eyes examined woodwork, rug, furniture, bookcase, as if he expected to spy Chuck Lane lurking somewhere in them.

'You're here all right,' she said. 'But Chuck isn't.'

'He isn't?' Ted considered that, drank deeply. Then, 'But your ex-husband is.'

'Earl dropped in to see Donnie.'

Ted drank again, and his glass was empty. Kay snatched it from him, danced into the kitchen for ice cubes. She danced back to mix another dark brown Scotch and soda.

Ted accepted it, drank absently. 'You and Chuck...you can tell *me* the truth, Mrs Lane. The two of you don't live together, do you.'

She saw a sheen in Ted's warm brown eyes. She saw their angle of vision. She saw his plump, freckled hands flex. She felt her breasts, hips, thighs suddenly examined, weighed. She said quickly, 'What on earth makes you think that? We do. Sometimes. And I wouldn't be surprised if...'

Ted, having begun an advance on her, came to a full stop. 'You live with him sometimes?' he asked mournfully.

'Sure. Most of the time.'

'Then when can I meet him?' Ted was all business again.

She pressed the advantage. 'I explained. He's a recluse. You can't ever meet him. Really. I mean that. I mean, he means that.'

Ted said, 'A smart woman like you, you ought to be able to change his mind, Mrs Lane. If you had any idea...'

'I have lots of ideas,' she said. 'And now...'

Ted stood his ground. He studied the living room. He gave ground. He moved into the hall. His brown eyes sought the kitchen, aimed toward the bedroom. They returned, so full of cloudy suspicion, that she expected him to charge bodily, through the rest of the house, to search from wall to wall. But at last, he gave ground again. He finished his drink, and conceded defeat. 'Okay, Mrs Lane. I hope you know what you're doing. I hope Chuck knows. But I tell you one thing. You tell him to call me. You tell him to get in touch with me right away. Now how about that? Isn't that fair enough? Isn't that reasonable? Isn't that...'

'It's possible,' she agreed, allowing him that small victory in hopes that it would take him on his way. 'I may be able to persuade Chuck to call you.' How, she didn't know. Who? What male? She would worry about that later.

'Is that a promise?' Ted pressed his luck.

Another small concession. 'It's a promise.'

'You won't forget?'

'Could I possibly forget this day?'

'Maybe not. So he'll call me?'

'Who?'

Ted's round face was full of pain. 'Chuck. Chuck Lane.' Then Ted's round face became full of suspicion. 'You seem to think it's a joke.'

'Not a bit,' she said fervently.

'Then he will call?'

She drew herself up. 'I promised.'

'When?'

She became cagey. 'It's going to take a few days. I have to reach him first.'

'He's far away?' Ted moved closer.

She said hastily, 'Oh, not far. But...'

'And you'll explain about the Galen thing, hunh? I mean...I wouldn't want him to misunderstand. I mean, there's nothing at all funny about it, only...'

'Chuck, if anyone in this world, would surely understand,' Kay assured Ted.

The last she saw of him, finally, was a back bowed in defeat, a head ducked down against April breeze, a short unwilling step that took him away into the twilight. It occurred to her then that she ought to have phoned a cab for him, lest he wander all night in the wilderness of Greenhill. It occurred to her, but she didn't call him back.

Instead, she plunged into the kitchen, intending to forget her troubles in house-wifely chores and motherly attentions.

Earl returned just as she was forming hamburger patties, forming them with the quick, crushing motions of millstones in the hands of the gods. She answered the door with blood on her fingers, beef-blood, rage in her heart, real rage, and fire in her amber eyes.

Earl said, 'Look. I want to know about this. What was that guy talking about anyhow? I mean, didn't he call me...I mean, not my name. But something else. Lane? I thought I heard him call me Lane.'

From Sandra, Kay had learned the value of a good offence. She immediately attacked. She cried, 'Earl Barrenger, if you and Sandra ever use Donnie, me, this place, as an excuse for a quick little get-together, I swear, I swear I will, Earl, I'll call the police, and I'll charge you both with trespassing, or breaking and entering, or snooping, or whatever the charge is. Do you have any idea of what Michael Devlin

271

could do, if I made a report like that to the police? Do you think you'd ever see Donnie again? Ever? Ever? Do you suppose that anybody in Greenhill would...'

Earl fell back, paling, hurt, bewildered, his honour impugned. He also fell back distracted. 'Why, Kay, I never...never...we didn't...how could you think?'

'Donnie said.'

'But Donnie's a kid. He doesn't understand. Sandra and I...I mean...we only meant.'

'Donnie is six years old. He is a capable and literate witness. Just remember that. And now, you get away! Beat it! Take off, Earl Barrenger!'

She slammed the door on a wailed protest.

She swaggered back to the kitchen. She plunged her hands into hamburger. But her sense of victory immediately died. There was still the small matter of putting Ted Blake in touch with Chuck Lane. If the two of them didn't at least speak together, she would, Kay knew, be at the mercy of Ted's continual harassment. New York was too close. Blake's interest too intense. Something would have to be done. But what?

Donnie had dinner.

She read to him for a little while. He was disposed to discuss the mysteries of THIS spelling this. She was disposed to think only of her problems. But she didn't have time to.

Donnie was no sooner asleep, than Sandra called to remind her that the Thespians were meeting. Sandra's approach was, 'Sorry I missed you today. I dropped in to tell you that we're getting together tonight. And Earl was visiting with Donnie. But you were so late...'

Kay accepted that as breezily as it was offered. She was, in fact, grateful to Sandra, whose earlier presence had, after all, had the lingering effect of arranging that cross fire of excited comment which distracted Earl and Donnie from hearing plainly Ted Blake's joyful expostulations.

She agreed that she would drop everything, grab Margery's costume, and hustle over in time to join the Thespians. Sewing for them was better than stewing at home, she informed herself.

Lee Berg, arriving after her call, was disposed to discuss some problems related to his newly-acquired love life. She

273

promised him a full, but future, session.

She arrived at the community centre breathless, and as usual, late, to be greeted by Ralph Parlmeyer's reproachful, 'This is awful, Kay. The show must go on. I rely on your help.'

She noted that she still understood him without translation. She noted that he no longer bore signs of Dick's attack. She noted that he was distraught.

She finally asked, not very kindly, how she could help him.

He said mournfully. 'With your vast powers of persuasion...'

'Me?'

'You, Kay.'

'Vast powers of persuasion?'

'Absolutely.'

Sandra sidled up in time to offer explanations. 'You see, Kay, Margery's dropped out of the production, and...'

Kay grinned, 'Forget it.' She stopped grinning. 'The costume.'

Sandra looked smug. 'I just happen to know the lines, Kay. I've explained to Ralph, explained carefully, that I can do the part.'

'The costume...' Kay moaned.

'You can make it smaller, can't you? Of

course it would have to be a lot smaller.' Willowy Sandra preened.

'But Margery...' Ralph insisted.

'I'll get you fitted right now,' Kay told Sandra, and did, and in a little while, Sandra linked her arm through Ralph's, and drew him away, whispering throatily.

Kay settled down with needle, thread, and thimble. A new plot began in her head. She told herself crossly to stop thinking like Chuck Lane. But still, there it was. Poor Ralph, poor Earl, and, of course, Poor Michael.

But, when Kay saw him the next day, Michael seemed to be perfectly all right.

He greeted her in a businesslike manner, ignoring the hopeful look she cast at the closed door of Mr Aker's office.

Mr Aker had returned, of course, but Michael plainly had no intention of turning her problem over to him. Certainly not while it afforded him the pleasure of continual amusement.

He said now, smiling, 'Further questions, Kay? I thought we had everything safely settled and arranged.'

'Except for one small thing. Chuck Lane himself.'

'Of course. What else? Tell me what's wrong.'

She explained.

Michael laughed.

She explained again, more firmly.

Michael laughed.

She didn't mind being the source of so much amusement, but she herself was not amused. She considered giving him an unedited version of the edited version she had given him before. She might induce him to stop laughing by telling him about Sandra's presence in the house just before Ted Blake's arrival. She restrained herself with the thought that she wanted him to concentrate on *her* problems. Instead, she told him what she thought had to be done.

He immediately stopped laughing. He refused. He didn't think that he could do an appropriate, nor convincing, Chuck Lane. He had a distinct impression, even more, an absolute conviction, that it might not be legal to pretend to be Chuck Lane. He felt that he definitely had to consider all angles of such an approach carefully. Much more carefully than Kay had apparently considered them.

She spoke quickly, earnestly, urgently,

and at last, desperately. It was essential that she produce a Chuck Lane for Ted Blake to talk to. He, Michael, was the only man she would trust to do the job. She amended quickly. To do *that* job. She...

Michael continued to talk until she rose, saying, 'Well, I guess I'd better take this whole thing to Mr Aker. You've told him about it anyway, haven't you?'

Michael sighed, and reached for the phone.

Sweet sweet silence.

The coffee, strong and hot, waited. The pencils were arranged. The portable was set up.

Kay slouched in her chair, smiling.

Michael, she thought, should have been in the Thespians along with Sandra. He was definitely an actor, an actor through and through. He made an exemplary Chuck Lane. If she had cast him from hundreds, she couldn't have found a better Chuck Lane.

It was a delight to review *his* end of the conversation with Ted Blake. It showed that he had an extraordinary grasp of the part. It was a true delight. She reviewed it.

Michael: 'This is Chuck Lane. I heard you've been hanging around, butting in, making passes at my wife. Now look, I'll say this once, and once is all. I'm a big, broad-minded guy, but that's one thing I'm not broad-minded about. I mean my wife. Kay. And you coming around here, making passes at her. I tell you, that burns me up. So what do you think you're up to?'

Ted Blake's replies were not hearable, nor did they matter. Kay happily dismissed them.

Michael: 'Yeah? Well, here it is, and on the line. I'm not interested in publicity. And I've got my reasons. My reasons are good enough for me. And if my wife thinks you were making passes at her, then you were. She ought to know. You bother her anymore, you come hanging around here, making goo-goo eyes, I find myself somebody else. Simple. I write. You sell. That's all there is. Bother me, I write, and somebody else sells. Sure. Sure. You're welcome. Pleasure to talk to you, too. Only don't expect me to talk to you every week. I've got other things to do. Sure. Sure. You're welcome.' Bang went the phone. Flash went Michael's grin...

Kay's fingertips hovered over the portable and then came down. *Helen went astride Earl. He moaned as their bodies joined. He writhed and she leaned over him, her sweet warm weight holding him, her thighs enclosing his, locked eager, demanding. His hands settled at her hips, fingers clenching into the soft flesh. They moved together, then separately, and suddenly they were a single striving, a quivering, a great gulping hunger in which they were devoured together. Sated, they became two again. Her cheek pressed to his heaving chest, Helen listened to the slowing thunder of his heart, and smiled.*

Donnie yelled, 'Mo-ther! Are you practising again?'

CHAPTER 16

Cupid Plots

'I don't understand it,' Cynthia said. 'Really, Kay, it seems to me that your father, lately—'

Sweet Cynthia, pink, plump, and just

slightly blowsy.

Kay nodded sympathetically, but without enthusiasm. She was making lists in her mind, and thinking ahead to all she had to do, wanted to do. She found it difficult to muster real concern for Cynthia, yet good manners, if not curiosity, demanded that she offer a listening ear.

Sweet Cynthia went on earnestly, 'I just have the feeling that your father...well, he talks about Amanda so much. I mean, really, Kay, that's hardly good taste, is it? To talk about Amanda? And to me?'

'Good taste?' Kay repeated, smoothing her red-gold bangs. 'Well, I don't know. Isn't it usual, Cynthia?'

'I don't know either,' Cynthia wailed. 'How would I know? He never did it before. We had our little days, our Tuesdays, our Thursdays, and he was so...so...Kay, you are a grown woman, married, divorced, you're so understanding. Kay, you tell me.' Cynthia's sugary voice became shrill with anguish. 'You tell me what's the matter with James.'

'Maybe it's just a mood,' Kay offered.

'It's lasting so long,' Cynthia wailed.

And the visit was, too, Kay thought, with a veiled, but desperate, glance at her wrist watch. 'I don't know,' she said finally. 'Perhaps...' She stopped.

'Perhaps?' Cynthia breathed, suddenly all hope and joy. 'Yes, Kay, dear. Perhaps what?'

But Kay's attention had been completely diverted by her own thoughts. The book.

Dear Dorrie, always a name, a hovering presence before, suddenly became a pink-fleshed reality. Chuck Lane was going to find it hard indeed to maintain her, as planned, in a subsidiary role. *Dear Dorrie* cried aloud to be expanded.

'Kay...' Cynthia's wail sirened through the mist of Chuck Lane's concentration. 'Kay, there's somebody at the door!'

Kay rose, grateful for the interruption.

She was no longer grateful when she found Earl on the steps. 'Donnie is not home now, Earl. As you ought to have known if you'd thought about it.'

'I did think about it.' Earl gave her an Earl look out of Earl blue eyes. 'I've been thinking...'

'Don't you ever go to work?'

'Don't change the subject.' Then, 'I've been thinking. Who was that red-headed guy hanging around here that day? Why did he call me...'

'None of your business.'

'But maybe it is.'

'I shall take this opportunity to remind you that you are hanging around here too much. Visiting privileges do not extend to the point you've been stretching them. Particularly since it is Sandra, and not Donnie that you've been visiting.'

'Listen...' Earl aggrieved was Earl familiar. 'Listen, Kay, you oughtn't to take Donnie seriously. He gets mixed up.'

'Not as mixed up as you do.'

Earl aggrieved was Earl angry. 'If you think you can get away with it, you have another think coming.'

'Get away with what?'

'I'm not going to stand out here on the steps and discuss our business, our son, your wild behaviour, in front of the whole neighbourhood.'

Kay made a careful survey of the street. She saw no one. She said so.

'That red-haired guy. He called me...he called me Lane, didn't he?'

'Come on in,' Kay said, stepping back.

Earl looked surprised, then mollified. That, to Kay, was another familiar expression. It meant that he thought he had gotten his own way, always soothing balm to his soul.

He said, 'Anyhow, we can talk inside,' and, 'You sure have fixed this place up,' as if he were an invited guest. And then, as if he belonged there, 'How about a cup of coffee?'

Kay restrained herself. She gritted her teeth, but managed to produce a smile. 'Sure, Earl. Come along to the kitchen. Just happens it's all ready.'

So was Sweet Cynthia. She straightend up, smiled, trilled, 'Oh, Kay, I didn't know you were expecting a man. I'd better go.'

Earl smiled, mumbled boyishly. Oh, he was so good at being boyish, Kay thought. 'I didn't mean to interrupt anything, Kay. I can come back later.'

Kay smiled over gritted teeth, and made casual introductions.

Earl and Sweet Cynthia seemed somehow very glad to meet each other.

Kay served them coffee while they chatted about the weather, growing spring was lovely, wasn't it? Greenhill, Rosemont, oh, Cynthia never went *there*, the Devlins, whom Cynthia just *adored*, Kay, her house, and finally, a lounge in town where good old-fashioned rock and roll was still played, and you could hardly hear that any more.

At long last, diverted Earl and comforted Sweet Cynthia departed together, repairing, Kay was certain, to that much-discussed lounge in town, and she for one wished them great joy of it and in each other.

They left, at last, and not a moment too soon, for not a deep breath after they had disappeared down the lane, James Mason arrived.

He was ruffled and restless. He announced that he could only stay for a little while. That he had just dropped in to see how Kay was getting along. That Mr Aker had mentioned her visit to Aker and Devlin, and stupid bastard, had refused to say why she had been there. As if he, James Mason, didn't have a right to know what kind of trouble his daughter was in. And when pressed, that stupid bastard Aker confessed that he actually didn't know either. The Devlin son-in-law, who played at being an attorney, and couldn't be trusted out of sight, that boy, had handled it for Kay, and he, old Aker, hadn't a clue...

Kay reheated the coffee without being asked for it. She wondered why her house was a way-station for the troubled, and listened without comment.

James ran down. He sat at the table, drumming his fingers.

She gave him hot coffee, said, 'Have some, Earl.'

James twitched. James subdued his twitch. He absently smoothed his hair, absently crossed and then re-crossed his legs. He said, 'That fool, that Earl, you just called me by his...'

Kay thought of Earl and Sweet Cynthia together. She said hastily, 'A ridiculous slip of the tongue.'

'Significant?' Then, thoughtfully, James went on, 'He's been hanging around here a lot, hasn't he? You're not planning to remarry him, are you?'

She shuddered, 'Hardly. But didn't you used to think that maybe I should?'

James looked surprised. 'Did I? It doesn't seem likely! Well, if that's not on your mind, what does he want around you?'

'He says it's to see Donnie.'

James let his face show what he thought of that.

Kay let her face agree. Then she went on. 'I am fairly certain that that particular

285

interest on his part is a thing of the past.'

James sighed, gave the kitchen a searching glance.

'Anything I can get for you?'

'Has your mother been here, Kay?'

'Not today.'

Kay waited.

'Moody lately. Have you noticed?'

'Just a little. It happens sometimes.'

'We were going to meet for lunch. She didn't show up.'

'Really? That's not like her.'

'I was there. Absolutely on time. Early even. Just as we'd arranged. And you haven't seen her?'

'Nope.'

'She's up to something. I can tell.'

'You're sure you're not imagining it?'

'Me?'

'Well, you could be, you know,' Kay assured him.

He looked unconvinced, and unconvinced he left.

It seemed to Kay a very good time to go out. If she weren't at home, no one could stop in to see her. And she could even put the time to good use. She went over the list she had written in her head while listening to Sweet Cynthia wail, and having gone over it, committed it carefully to a scrap of paper.

The scrap of paper was still on the kitchen table when she drove away.

The drugstore was steamy, heated for February instead of for April. Kay stood in front of the cash register, and fanned herself, and cleared her throat.

Mr Avis, reared up, red-faced and irate. 'Always in a hurry. Can't wait a minute. That's what's wrong with the world.' Then he smiled, warmed. 'Oh, Mrs Barrenger, it's you! Just reading a little.' He held up a book. 'See this one yet? *Doing It.* Hot, I tell you. And real. That fool Mrs Planter...' He stopped, 'What would you like?'

Kay opened her mouth, closed it. The list was at home. Unfortunately, she didn't remember what she had written on it.

He was patient, but bewildered. 'Yes?'

'I'm afraid I forgot.'

That delighted him. 'Happens all the time. Just wander around, have a good look. It'll come to you. It'll just jump out...'

What jumped out was Amanda.

She came from between the paperback racks, with a book clutched in her hand.

'That you, Kay? I thought I heard your voice,' and then, 'Wait a minute.' She vanished behind the racks again and returned empty-handed.

The oddly guilty look on her face made Kay curious.

Amanda said, 'Mr Avis, don't you have any fudgsicles?' as Kay started for the rack.

He said it was too early, and suggested a chocolate ice cream sandwich.

Amanda's refusal sounded shocked. 'I want a fudgsicle, Mr Avis.'

Kay edged around her, ducked close to the paperbacks.

The Hot Stars by Chuck Lane.

Adventuring by Chuck Lane

Loving by Chuck Lane

Doing It by Chuck Lane.

Sold out, but back. Returned to the public's eye. And a very nice display. Kay scanned it, but with satisfaction, and pride. Was Amanda studying them? And if so, why?

Amanda, at her shoulder, said, 'I can't find anything to read.'

There were dozens of books. Spy stories. Mystery stories. Love stories. Baby books. Travel books. How-to-do books of every kind. 'There's enough to choose from,' Kay told Amanda.

'Nothing touches me,' Amanda complained. Then, 'Let's go get me a fudgsicle.'

Kay suddenly remembered what had headed her list. She bought a huge bottle of aspirin. She resignedly followed Amanda past the barbershop, sneaking a glimpse at the offices of the *Greenhill Sentinel* above it, and through the shopping centre. Kay suggested several times that she had things to do. Amanda could easily carry on alone. But Amanda clung, and once she had found her fudgsicle, she licked it contentedly, suggesting, with hardly concealed guile, 'Let's go home and go through your basement, Kay.'

'Go through my basement?' Kay echoed. 'What for?'

'I don't know. It's a good day for it.'

'Start in your own house.'

Amanda shrugged, tipped her silver-blond head back. 'Yours is more likely.'

'Likely for what?'

'I don't know.' Amanda finished her fudgsicle with a sigh, licked her fingers, looked as if she were about to say she wanted another.

Kay, watching, made bets with herself. But suddenly the avid look on Amanda's face changed. She beamed, 'Oh, hello, hello, there,' and reached out both hands in greeting.

Jonathan seized her hands, smiled first at her, then at Kay. Kay kept her hands firmly at her side. She kept them very firmly there, because they had an odd itch to smooth his ruffled hair, to straighten his askew tie, to...

He finally let go of Amanda's, and surreptitiously wiped damp fudgsicle from his fingers. 'Out shopping ladies?'

Kay nodded.

Amanda said, 'Not really. And we're tired. Doesn't hot coffee sound good?' Kay said quickly, 'I have to get home.'

Amanda said just as quickly, 'Nonsense,' and swept an unwilling Kay, a very willing Jonathan, into the Do-Nut Shoppe. Having done that, and settled herself, and them, chattering brightly, Amanda suddenly paused. She had spied Sandra, sitting alone in a corner.

Amanda gathered herself instantly. 'Now you two sit right here. I'll just go say hello. But don't you move. Let's see, order me...oh, order me a couple of doughnuts, will you?' Amanda darted away, crying, 'Sandra, oh, Sandra, dear. I'm, coming. Stay just where you are.'

Jonathan grinned at Kay. 'I guess you're stuck with me.'

'Just wait,' she said, once more making bets with herself. And she was winner. Sandra rose, met Amanda halfway. Sandra somehow managed to out-manoeuvre Amanda. Within moments, Jonathan was completely surrounded. Women to the right of him, women to the left of him, women in front of him. He seemed to enjoy it. He ordered coffee and doughnuts all around.

Amanda gobbled hers down, and licked her fingers, and artlessly asked for two more.

Sandra passed hers across to Amanda. 'If you insist, but really, I do think you ought to be careful, Amanda, you know, at your age...' Long dark eyes suddenly narrowed. 'As a matter of fact, it seems to me that you're putting on a little weight.'

Amanda's blue-green eyes narrowed, too. She said sweetly, 'It's so aging to be haggard, you know. And then,' she turned to Jonathan, 'our civilization is so...so odd, don't you think? We are mentally destroying ourselves by trying to remain children. By children I mean trying to remain adolescents. Women these days, they just refuse to grow up. They...'

Kay choked.

Jonathan grinned.

Amanda finished her sentence calmly. 'They even, yes, they even think that child-bearing is beneath them.'

Sandra squirmed.

Sandra paled. She obviously considered the subject indelicate. She said, to Jonathan, 'You mustn't forget to see the Thespians' play.'

He said he wouldn't forget it.

She said, 'Ralph Parlmeyer is the lead. The English professor from the university, you know. A very virile type...'

'Virile,' Amanda put in. 'Oh, now really, is that all you can say for him? I mean, really, Sandra, virility...'

'Is necessary if women are going to have babies,' Kay put in.

Amanda glanced at her watch, rose. 'Come on, Sandra. We have things to do.'

'I,' Sandra retorted, 'do not have things

to do. I have only one thing. Which is to get my hair taken care of.'

'If you do persist in spending your time at trivial affairs,' Amanda said pityingly, every silver-blond hair in place, 'then what can I do?'

Sandra was on her feet, undaunted, though defeated. She beat Amanda out the door by three steps and two critical comments.

Jonathan wiped his brow. 'I was afraid, for a minute, that...'

'They're good friends,' Kay said.

Jonathan looked dubious, but let it go. He said, 'And so, thanks to your mother, we're alone. So I want to tell you...don't you think we could start over again some way?'

'What for?'

'I don't kick dogs. I'm a pretty careful driver.'

'Excellent recommendation.' Prickles prickled along her arms. Her legs felt unaccountably weak. She noticed an ink stain near his collar.

His deep voice drawled silkily, 'Well, let's see. More than that. I'm free, over twenty-one, fairly intelligent, fairly personable, I like kids...'

'I think that's very nice.' She pushed her coffee cup aside. 'But I'm pretty busy these days.'

His lean face tightened. 'I can believe that, all right. When you're not turning in false fire alarms, you're tangled up with your ex-husband, and that Jersey talking English professor, and that kook Sam Golden.'

'I see no reason for you to keep a dossier on me, Mr Williams,' she said icily, with the weakness in her knees having spread to her chest.

'I'm interested. That's a pretty good reason.'

'Thank you for the coffee,' she said politely, and rose, and stalked away leaving Jonathan quite alone, having suffered first the feast, now facing the famine. From too many women to no women.

She tried to concentrate on that very Chuck Lane kind of thought as she headed for the door. But from behind her, drawling voice raised irritably, he called, in full hearing of the Do-Nut Shoppe's eagerly attending ears, 'I was just trying to ask you how about a date, Kay Barrenger! Don't act as if I threatened to rape you!'

CHAPTER 17

Stormy Weather

The next day presented Kay with a series of small and not so small shocks.

First, Mr Fairbanks banged on her door, thrust the mail at her, and seemed disposed to linger while she gave quick, nonchalant, half-glances at the several return addresses. Among them, along with the bank's, the local department store's, the garage's, all bills, of course, was one that seemed to glow in her hand, to flash at her, signalling trouble, trouble, trouble ahead. Britanica Company, Inc. Sent directly to her house! It took her a moment to register the fact that the name on it was Mrs Earl Barrenger. It took her another moment to catch her breath and reassure herself that it could be nothing more than a follow-up on her query of two years before. Meanwhile, fat Mr Fairbanks, disposed to linger and chat, was saying, 'How're things with you, Mrs Barrenger? Had any company lately?

What's doing with that cousin of yours? What was his name? Let me see, now it was...something...just on the tip of my tongue.'

She hastily suggested that Mr Fairbanks might want to come in for tea or coffee or something. He agreed that a cup of tea would do him nicely. 'You must be a mind reader, Mrs Barrenger. A mind reader, that's what you are.'

At last, served tea, and diversion, he departed for his appointed rounds, and Kay made a whirlwind through the house, ruthless in chore-doing, in hopes of creating time for *her* appointed rounds. Which were many.

These were, as she had listed them: work from ten to two; dress from two to two-ten; meet Donnie's teacher for conference from two-fifteen to...? Then, home, dinner, Donnie; and at last, work from nine to...?

The second shock, a not so small one, was presented through the medium of the telephone. Donnie's teacher, slightly acid, but pretending concern, called to ask if Mrs Barrenger had forgotten their consultation.

'But our confrontation...' Kay choked on

the slip of the tongue, her wail silenced only momentarily, and then, resuming, 'It was for two-fifteen, wasn't it?'

'Ten-fifteen,' the teacher told her, highly acid, and no longer concerned.

'I'll be right there,' Kay promised.

She arrived breathless, and unprepared. The intelligent parent was, of course, expected to ask all sorts of intelligent questions. She was not only unprepared. She was decidedly unprepossessing. Her bright bangs were plastered to her forehead. Her shirt and jeans clung to her. Her sneakers tracked water across the polished floor. For as she stepped out of her car, the April sky had grumbled and turned dark, and the April breeze had sharpened and an April shower had beset her.

She carefully mopped her face, and rearranged her wet bangs. She carefully caught her breath. She made her apologies, and then waited.

The somewhat frazzled teacher looked at her.

Kay gave in. 'Donnie's doing okay, isn't he?'

The teacher continued to look at her.

'He's a very bright boy!' Then, 'Isn't he?'

'He's bright. No doubt about that.' The teacher was oddly grim.

'But...?' Alarm signals, angry pulses. Kay felt them, reminded herself to be coolly amused.

'He does remarkably well with reading and vocabulary.' Then still oddly grim, the teacher went on. 'But he is a problem in class. He has an obsession.'

'A what!'

'With practising. Are you by any chance studying the piano, Mrs Barrenger?'

'Typing,' Kay said succinctly.

'Typing.' The teacher was thoughtful. 'That *is* what Donnie told me. I thought he was confused.'

'Donnie doesn't get confused.'

'Perhaps you're writing a book,' the teacher suggested, having her small joke.

Kay didn't smile, nor respond.

'I thought not,' the teacher said quickly. 'Then you must be thinking of taking a job. You know, if at all possible, Mrs Barrenger, it would be best not to. We do find that the children of working mother...'

Kay had to halt the even flow of perfectly pronounced words. The teacher was obviously off on some lecture she had prepared long before, and given often. Kay allowed her wet purse to fall from her wet lap. She swooped to retrieve it. She rose red-faced and breathless again. 'I have as much to do now as I can manage.'

'Good. Now about Donnie's obsession... we always value the children's ob...I should say...suggestions. In Greenhill we believe that every child is a small human being, a functioning mechanism, an intellect, a personality, in its own right. But...'

'But...?' Kay, wary, waited.

'Donnie insists we practise. Everything. For more time than we can spare.'

'It doesn't do any harm, does it?'

'Delaying orderly procedure,' the teacher murmured. Then, brightening, 'Of course. You and your...that is, Donnie is the product of a broken home, isn't he? Perhaps...'

'My typing,' Kay said. 'Not my ex-husband has produced this extremely dangerous and asocial behaviour in Donnie. I'll see what I can do.'

'A normal home has two parents, Mrs Barrenger.'

Kay rose. 'I'll see what I can do,' she repeated.

She decided that she would have to start teaching Donnie to be more tolerant. Some people practised a lot, and some didn't.

Satisfied that she had found the proper approach, she returned home, revising her mental list. From eleven to four, work.

She set up, and settled down.

Dear Dorrie didn't like being the other woman, not when her lover made her feel as if she were his wife, and his wife his new and beloved mistress. Hurt pride, and hunger, made her eager in Earl's arms. (The new book, as yet unnamed.)

Arms. Arms. Arms.

Kay suffered her third shock of the day. Arms...prickles on her skin. She was, instead of working, thinking of Jonathan. His deep, drawling voice...his wide shoulders...his tousled russet hair...his... Chuck Lane had no business thinking of Jonathan Williams.

She could have gone to the movies with him. It wouldn't have meant anymore than going out with Sam Golden, or Ralph Parlmeyer, or any of the other possibilities trotted out by Amanda...Amanda, who, it suddenly occurred to Kay, hadn't trotted out any possibilities lately. Who, it also occurred to Kay, seemed oddly different. And who, as Kay sat considering her, arrived.

She came, without knocking, without calling ahead, into the kitchen. She came and sat tiredly in a chair.

Her arrival was the fourth shock. Kay rose, prickles and Jonathan completely forgotten, in quick alarm. Chuck Lane was at work at the table. The yellow pages were spread...

But Amanda arrived not only unannounced, but also unobservant. She asked plainly not noticing the litter on the table, the portable. Kay's frantic expression, 'You busy, Kay?' and sighed. And added, 'Hand me a cracker from the cookie bin, will you?'

'Not busy,' Kay said through her teeth, producing crackers from the pantry after stowing the portable away, pouring coffee from the stove, after casually shuffling the loose yellow sheets into a pile, and putting them on the yellow dishwasher. 'Not busy at all.'

Amanda sipped coffee, frowned, sighed again.

Kay abandoned her mental list for the moment, the day, perhaps the week. 'Something wrong?'

Amanda sipped, smiled. 'Oh, no. It's wonderful.'

'What is it?'

'Haven't you heard? I thought everybody in Greenhill knew.'

'Knew what?'

'Of course I wish it were you, Kay. You can't imagine how I worry about you.'

'But what?'

'Oh. Margery. She's pregnant again.'

'Poor Dick.'

'He's delighted. Men are always delighted.' Then, 'I do so wish it were you though.'

'It might be embarrassing. Since I don't have a husband.'

'But you should. This running around with different men. That's Sandra's style perhaps. But it's not yours, it's...'

Kay stared. 'Are you all right?'

'Of course. The doctor says I'm in perfect condition.'

'Perfect condition,' Kay echoed.

'For my condition, that is,' Amanda added.

'Your condition. Listen, are you...'

'The way things are now, you really ought to...'

'Mo-ther! Are you...?'

Amanda answered simply. 'Yes. I am.' At Kay's astounded look, Amanda went on, 'It is not unheard of. I am a young woman after all. And your father is a...'

'Wonderful,' Kay cried.

'Isn't it?' Amanda beamed. 'Except for Sweet Cynthia. Just wait until she hears.'

'Oh, I wouldn't worry about Sweet Cynthia,' Kay retorted, thinking of Earl.

She forgot him quickly, for Amanda rose, intent on scavenging in the basement for Donnie's outgrown baby things. Kay considered the basement, with its neatly-labelled boxes of author's copies, and final carbons, all tucked in among stuffed animals and infant blankets and old canning jars, to be completely out of bounds. She prepared to argue. But she didn't have to.

James said from the doorway, 'Amanda, dear, you ought to be ashamed! Here I was, calling you at home, expecting you to answer, and no one did, and I thought...dear God, you can't imagine what awful things I thought...You must learn to take care of yourself.' He took Amanda's arm tenderly. 'Consider your condition.'

They left together, arm in arm, Amanda's silver-blond head held proudly high, her slim feet taking careful steps, while James strutted joyfully beside her.

Kay considered the various pregnancies in her family, and decided that it was probably a good thing that she hadn't been swayed into any man's arms in that period of fertility. She found herself, much to her disgust, once again thinking of Jonathan.

She immediately brought out the portable, rescued the yellow sheets from the dishwasher. She reread what she had done thus far, reread again, and continued to think of Jonathan.

Donnie came home, and asked for cookies. There were no cookies.

Relieved, Kay cleared the kitchen, and then baked. She discussed tolerance with Donnie. He agreed that people should only practise when, and how much, they wanted to. She hoped that at some time in the future she wouldn't regret having suggested that much tolerance to him.

She cooked dinner. She read with Donnie.

The phone rang. Sandra, a throaty whisper, 'Kay, dear? When do you expect to deliver my costume?'

Kay was airy. 'Oh, it's just about ready, Sandra. Anytime now.' At which point she received the fifth shock.

'Anytime just happens to be now. Right

304

now. Dress rehearsal is about to start. I want to get ready.'

'Now?'

'Kay...'

Kay said hastily. 'In a minute.'

She didn't waste time trying to remember if she had been told about the dress rehearsal. She didn't waste time taking those last few but decidedly necessary stitches. She called Lee Berg. He wasn't at home. She called Rick's mother. She was entertaining. She called Amanda. Amanda was sorry, but in her condition...Sam Golden was out. Sweet Cynthia was expecting Earl momentarily. And so it went. At last, in desperation, Kay called Jonathan. He was working late. He had nothing to do but work late. Sure. He'd be right over.

By the time he arrived, only moments later, the few but necessary stitches were in. He assured her that he could move fast even when the house wasn't burning down. He also assured her that he would not deliver the costume to Sandra. If he went, he would have to sit through the dress rehearsal. He had to see the play at opening night. Two performances was two too many. He would baby-sit while she delivered the costume. Donnie appeared to investigate. Jonathan amended the baby-sitting to entertaining. Donnie appeared delighted. Jonathan was delighted. Kay left for the community centre, costume over her arm, sweat on her brow, and prickles all over her.

Sandra, in black lace, her own, was clasped in Ralph's arms.

Kay prepared to leave, but was talked into staying. Her services would be necessary if the costume fell apart.

The rehearsal went as such rehearsals always go.

When the curtain fell on the third act, Sandra was sweet and importunate. 'Are you sure it fits as it should, Kay? I'm afraid it's a bit too loose.'

Kay disagreed.

'And it won't fall apart?' Sandra still sweet, still smiling, her long dark eyes full of secrets.

'I don't think so,' Kay assured her.

'Funny thing about Earl,' Sandra mused. 'I'd never have thought he went for fattish middle-aged women.'

'He goes for all women.'

'Earl,' Sandra mused sweetly. 'Earl, Earl, Earl.' She grinned broadly. 'Tell me the truth, Kay. Is he as bad, really? Or should I say as good, as you make him out to be?'

The sixth shock.

Kay played dumb. She widened her amber eyes. She raised her dimpled chin. 'What?'

'And how soon,' Sandra purred, 'will you be going to Rosemont, to the post office?'

Kay played dumber, both ways, silent and stupid. But she thought of Michael, the various ways in which she would repay him for his perfidy.

Sandra seemed to pick the thought out of her mind. 'Kay, dear, you mustn't blame Michael. Blame yourself. A sheet of yellow paper under the kitchen table. Earl and June and...'

'I have to get home,' Kay said.

'Such a busy girl. I quite understand.' Sandra turned to smile at Ralph who had come to join the two women. 'Taking me home, Ralph, dear?' she purred.

'I'll just get your coat. Not a minute. I have a terrible thirst.' And to Kay, 'We have to talk it all over, you know. Before tomorrow night.'

'I know,' she said tranquilly, and when

Ralph had hurried away. 'Sandra, you want to watch him. He drowns himself in Martinis. And Michael...' Kay paused delicately. It was never necessary to use too heavy a hand with Sandra. Kay went on then, 'And Michael is so fastidious. I don't imagine that he and Ralph...'

Sandra laughed. 'Such gentle blackmail, Kay. Never mind. I ask only one thing. I love knowing authors. One of these days, you must get Chuck Lane to autograph his books for me.'

Driving toward the safety of home, Kay considered. Would Sandra broadcast what she knew? Had the Ralph-Michael hint been successful? Considered, and decided. Sandra not only *loved* knowing an author. She also *loved* having secrets.

In the warmth of her relief, Kay forgot that Jonathan would be waiting for her return.

She trotted into the house, thinking ahead. The still unnamed book...

Jonathan said, 'Well, how did it go?'

She told him that he would be seeing a great play the next night. He seemed doubtful.

She thanked him for helping her.

He seemed pleased.

She made a very large tired yawn.

He seemed disposed to stay.

She gave in, made coffee, and small talk, and finally, she thanked him several more times for helping her out. He took the hint at last, and preparing to depart, he shook her hand.

It was a nice, old-fashioned, formal gesture.

She liked it.

He shook her hand, and she shivered.

There was something definitely *there*.

She forgot about the portable, the yellow sheets. She forgot Earl, Dear Dorrie. She watched Jonathan stride into the shadows of the spring night, and wished he had insisted on staying.

Desolate and depressed, she went to bed.

She had the last shock of the day in her sleep.

She spent an extraordinary sex-filled night dreaming of Jonathan.

CHAPTER 18

Truths Win Out

'Turn about,' Jonathan said silkily, 'is fair play. I baby-sat for Donnie last night, didn't I?'

'Entertained him.'

'Entertained him?' Jonathan demurred. 'Not at all. He entertained me. Still...'

'But I don't know how to write a review of the show.'

'You don't even have to put in an appearance. You saw it last night.'

'I still don't know how to...'

'You're completely literate. And you've got to help me out.' Jonathan was firm. 'Things have come up. The P.T.A, that committee of yours...'

To get him off the subject, Kay agreed that she would do the review. Then she promptly added, 'But it's not "that committee of mine." '

'I'll concede that. Okay? Call me tomorrow as soon as you're finished and

310

I'll pick it up.'

'I'll drop it by,' she said hastily.

'When?'

'I don't know when. As soon as it's ready.'

'But I might be out of the office,' he drawled.

Which was a consummation devoutly to be wished, Kay thought, and exactly what she was planning. All that went unsaid. What was said was, 'Goodbye, Jonathan.'

That was also what was meant.

She had it all worked out. She was, decidedly, not going to see any more of Jonathan Williams. She was, decidedly, tired of having prickles prickle her arms, and having a weakness in her legs, and certainly she was tired of ridiculous sexy-style dreams.

Chuck Lane had already complicated her life quite sufficiently. She did not intend to allow anyone else to complicate it further. She had asked a favour of Jonathan, because she was desperate for help. She wondered suddenly why she hadn't thought of calling her sister, or brother-in-law. Why she hadn't simply taken Donnie with her? Why she...never mind. She hadn't thought of those expedients at the moment. So she had asked a favour of Jonathan. And he, being Jonathan, was holding her to strict account, and demanding a favour back. But, once the review was done, delivered at lunchtime when he would surely not be there, she would be able to forget Jonathan Williams, prickles, houses burning down, and what was *there*. She would...

She would never promise to do anything for anybody ever again. She watched as Sandra melted into Ralph's arms. The curtain came down. The applause was prolonged, enthusiastic, and full of suburban forgiveness. Sandra came out, smiling. Ralph came out, beaming. The two of them came out together. The curtain came down once more, and remained down, and Kay joyfully rose to go.

Sam Golden surged through the crowded aisle to reach her side. 'My dear, Kay, how are you?' he demanded. He removed his horn-rim glasses and peered at her, then replaced them and peered at her. His eyes swept her up and down in careful inventory of her curves.

She wondered if she had, in an absent-minded moment, only *thought* of putting on her new red pique dress. She assured Sam that she was all right, but worried about the review she had promised to do for the *Greenhill Sentinel.*

'For the *Sentinel?*' Sam frowned. Then the frown cleared. Deep understanding took it's place. 'Oh, he's the man that threatened to rape you in the Do-Nut Shoppe, isn't he?'

Kay's vehement, and silent, denial did not deter Sam.

He went on, 'So that's why you came? I *was* surprised when I saw you.'

She told him that she was surprised at his surprise. After all, she had, with her own hands, sewn the outfit Sandra was wearing now originally for Margery and finally for Sandra herself. Kay had a vested interest in attending the performance. She had to be sure Sandra wasn't suddenly left virtually nude under the footlights in Ralph's arms.

Sam explained, as he carefully wiped steam off his glasses with a tent-size white linen handkerchief. 'You've pulled out of so many things, Kay. People have wondered.'

'They have?' She was puzzled. She didn't remember pulling out of anything.

'The P.T.A. The committee.' He beamed suddenly. 'And have you heard about our successes? Chuck Lane's books aren't going to be sold in Greenhill anymore. That is, not every place. Now you take Mr Avis. He is a reasonable man. When Mrs Planter tackled him for the third time... We've got them on the run, Kay. I do wish you were with us in our victory.'

She brushed her red-gold bangs off her brow. She raised her chin, her eyes, her voice. 'What are you talking about?'

'It's a big thing, bigger than I expected. We've even begun to get mail.' He looked a bit embarrassed. 'Some of it...well, it takes all kinds...'

'What if Chuck Lane sues you?'

Sam suddenly looked worried. 'How can he?'

'Aren't you interfering with his civil rights?'

'What?'

'Interfering with his pursuit of life, liberty, and happiness. Not to mention livelihood.'

'Certainly not!' Sam cried, drawing his pudgy self up.

But she had convinced herself, at least. Seething she bade Sam goodbye once more, and seething she went out to her car.

It looked as if a long night of labour stretched ahead of her.

Lee Berg said, 'You know that Mr Williams? Well, he called three times. Wanted to know if you were home yet. I told him no.'

'Thanks, Lee. And now...'

'Do you think he'll be coming over soon?'

'Certainly not. At this hour? Decent people go to bed. So you probably ought to...'

'I'd sure like to see him. For one thing he's a science fiction buff. Nobody around here ever reads a book hardly, much less science fiction. Besides...'

Against her better judgement, Kay prompted Lee. 'Besides what?'

He gave her a soulful look, a soulful and mature look. He sighed, 'Mrs Barrenger, you sure are...you are...well, you're really cool.'

She thanked him. She noticed that he had not responded to her prompting and took the coward's way out. She didn't press him.

'I wish that Mr Williams were coming

out here tonight. I've got to talk to him.'

'Why don't you stop by his office? It's over the barber shop in the shopping centre.'

'You know perfectly well I can't go to see him at his office. It would be just like if I went to see my father at *his* office. Can't you imagine?' Scorn fuelled him into his leather vest, fuelled him to the door.

Abashed, she said weakly, 'I'll tell him you want to talk to him, Lee. How about that?'

Lee whirled. 'Would you? And listen, explain it's about...it's about this friend of mine. He needs advice. He's in love, really really in love. With an older woman, Mrs Barrenger. And he...' Lee's acne-marked face was suddenly as red as Kay's dress. He finished with a rush, '...he doesn't know how to tell her. I've got to go, Mrs Barrenger.' He fought the door open, disappeared into the April night, a need looking for a comfort.

Kay sighed. She knew exactly how he felt. But she didn't know what to do about it. Either for him. Or for herself.

She faced the long night of labour ahead of her.

First, the review. She titled it, Thespians'

Triumph. It was short, sweet, gentle, signed Kay Barrenger. It took her half an hour. She reread it, making certain by checking the three pages against the programme, that she had managed to mention every listed name, plus a few she knew that hadn't been included. Jonathan's favour repaid, she set the review aside for delivery the next morning.

Second, a blistering letter to Samuel Golden, copy to the P.T.A Greenhill Elementary School, copy to the *Greenhill Sentinel.*

The blistering letter charged that Chuck Lane's rights as an author, a human being, a citizen, were being denied to him by the vigilante activities of the P.T.A committee to see about *those* books. He wrote, the publisher published, the bookstores sold. Nobody forced anybody to read Chuck Lane's work. Nobody had the right to prevent anybody else from reading it either. She signed it Chuck Lane. She signed all three copies, put them into envelopes, stamped them, and went out to mail them.

Then, the third item in her long night of labour...the still unnamed book.

The receptionist was very young, very

317

blond, very pretty. Entirely too young, blond, and pretty, in Kay's jaundiced view.

She had always assumed that Jonathan worked surrounded by cigar-smoking men in shirt sleeves, and small old ladies in pince nez.

Now exhausted by both her night's labours at the portable, and by her struggle to sleep in spite of inviting dreams, she soon discovered that the pretty, young, blond receptionist had a squint, unfortunate but obvious, a squeaky voice, and bowed legs showing beneath a too-short miniskirt. Kay made these kindly observations while she carefully put a big brown envelope on the desk and said, smiling brightly, 'For Mr Williams. The Thespians' play review. Will you see that he gets it?'

The receptionist's squeaky voice offered a chill, 'I'll do that little thing for you.'

Kay produced an equally chill, 'thanks,' and departed.

Instead of being coolly amused, she was hotly angry. Disappointment lodged like a cold hard-boiled egg in her throat. The least that Jonathan Williams, that boor, could do, was be in the office when he knew she would be stopping by. And it was ridiculous to have a newspaper office over a barbershop. The least he could do...

She was in the car when she heard the shout.

She peered out, saw nothing. She looked again. Jonathan stood in the door of the barbershop. His lean face was whiskered with white lather. He was swathed in white, the drape of a Roman toga.

She grinned, raised her hand in a salute, and drove away.

The highway to Rosemont was sun-filled. Lilacs bloomed. Birds sang. She felt somewhat soothed by the time she had parked the emerald-green hardtop in the parking area. She was somewhat more soothed when the post office clerk welcomed her warmly, appreciative eyes cataloguing her pink dress, as well as the form which filled it.

She checked her box. One letter. It was from Britanica Company, Inc. It said:

Dear Chuck:
I guess that's what you want to be called and that's okay with me. It doesn't matter if Mrs Earl Barrenger and you gave the same address in separate communications to us.
After all, lots of ladies like Mrs Earl

Barrenger have rooms for rent and stuff. So it makes sense you lived there. Okay? Satisfied? Happy? Bored *will be in the book stores in a couple of months. The publishers like small mysteries, so they're asking me questions and I'm giving them the answers you want me to give them. Okay? Satisfied? Happy? You should be. The publishers are happy too. They like* Society's Proprieties *a lot, and they'll publish it, also hardcover, with a big campaign, you mystery man, you. Advance enclosed. Note that you got a raise. Write soon.*

Warmest regards,
Galen Maradick

Kay grinned. There was apparently no more Ted Blake, just as there was no more Mrs Earl Barrenger. She must be sure to call and tell Michael.

She grinned harder. *Society's Proprieties* had sold, and hardcover. But, of course, the novel she was in the midst of would be the best, the most satisfying, of Chuck Lane's books, and would remain that until it was finished and a new one was begun.

Completely soothed she deposited part of the cheque in her Rosemont Chuck

Lane account. The rest she kept in cash. She had an unexplainable yen for a whole new outfit. She returned to Greenhill.

She did grocery shopping. Since the supermarket was two stores from Mr Avis' drugstore, with the barber shop between she passed the barber shop. No white whiskered Roman appeared to challenge her.

Mr Avis' shiny head, the top of it only, was visible behind the counter. He did not look up when she entered the store.

She went briskly to the paperback racks. She stalked the covers. No Chuck Lane. None. Not one. She went briskly to the counter. 'Mr Avis?'

He grunted, sighed, grumbled. At last he raised his head. His eyes brightened. 'How do you do, Mrs Barrenger?'

'I'm looking for...my...I mean...is it true that you've stopped carrying those books, the Chuck Lane books?'

Mr Avis shrugged. 'That's what you people want, isn't it? I mean...your committee...Mrs Planter. Though I must say, Mrs Barrenger, it surprised me that you, after all, you've bought...and you don't look like the type that...'

'It is not my committee. I am opposed to

vigilante action. I want you to stock those books, Mr Avis.'

He looked at her. He looked carefully around the empty store. He looked at the display window. 'Well, to tell you the truth, Mrs Barrenger...' he reached under the counter, brought up *Doing It,* '...to tell you the truth, I've got a bunch of them right here. Anybody that asks me...'

'They should be displayed, Mr Avis.'

'Well, you see...'

'You're not fearful of *those* people, are you?'

'Not exactly. But that Mrs Planter, she...'

She said severely, 'We must be brave in the defence of our liberties, Mr Avis.'

His beet-red face brightened with admiration. 'Say, Mrs Barrenger, now you put it that way.' He paused, thought, sighed. But then, with a sad and aching grunt, he stooped behind the counter. 'I'll do it,' he said. 'I will. No matter what happens.'

'And I'll help.'

When she left, the racks in Mr Avis' drugstore displayed *The Hot Stars, Doing It, Adventuring, Loving.*

With that victory behind her, she stopped to see Margery.

Amanda was there, too.

The two women briefly mentioned a letter Sam Golden had gotten. Something about a suit. Something about a Chuck Lane. They were very vague about it. They were much less vague smugly comparing yens, symptoms and sensations.

Kay was pointedly excluded. She was, after all, not pregnant. Not even married. Mother and sister made it quite clear that to be not pregnant, not even married, placed a woman beyond the pale, made her dull, a clod, unlovely, and obviously unlovable. Unaccountably, Kay's spirits flagged.

She returned home consoling herself with the thought of all the lovely black lace underwear she intended to buy. The consolation soured when she realized that no one would ever see it. The consolation sweetened again, when as she unloaded the groceries, she decided on the title of the unnamed book. It would be called simply, honestly, sincerely... *Hungry*. It would come out hardcover, and it would start out fifth on the bestseller list and climb to first and stay there for... The consolation soured. Nobody would know who Chuck Lane really was. Nobody but herself. Of course there were the Devlins, Michael and Sandra, but they didn't count. Their knowing didn't offer Kay that particular satisfaction to which she was entitled.

She slammed the refrigerator door on her hand, and yelped. Nobody came rushing to find out what had happened. She thrust her hand under the cold water faucet, and stood there, forgetting to turn it on. When she realized that, she burst into tears.

The telephone rang. She ignored it, but then, exasperated into action, she dashed to answer it. It went silent before she reached it. At that rebuff, she burst into tears again. Tears became flood, but even floods are finite. Drought finally ensued. She wiped her eyes and sought the only available anodyne for pain.

She curled up on the sofa, a book in her lap. Comforted, she opened it. Comforted, she read: *Doing It by Chuck Lane. Chapter 1.*

And that was when Jonathan arrived.

He pounded on the door, shouted, 'Kay Barrenger! Don't you ever stay home?' and the door bounced open.

'I am at home,' she said, coolly amused, and closing the book in her lap. 'But shouldn't you knock?'

She noted that he was very well-shaven. His russet hair was freshly-trimmed, and brushed, natural curl subdued. His tie was straight. Jacket and trousers matched, both of them still exuding steam-iron scent. He held crushed in one hand a sheet of yellow paper. She assumed that to be the copy of the Chuck Lane letter to the P.T.A CSTB. He held crushed in his other hand three sheets of white paper, which she assumed to be her play review. But among those three sheets of white paper, there were several of yellow. She did not know what to assume them to be.

'Shouldn't I knock?' he demanded, the deep warm drawl quickened by exasperation. 'How do I know what you'd do? You might call the fire department.'

'But why?' she asked sweetly, still eyeing those yellow sheets among the white. Eyeing them uneasily while faint suspicions began to rise like flickering silver fish in a disturbed stream.

'That's a good question. We'll get to it later.' And, as she rose, 'Sit down, Kay Barrenger! We have things to talk about.'

She sat down, partly because there was a sudden weakness in her legs, but mostly because he had put two big hands on her shoulders and pushed. She sat down with the crushed roll of yellow and white sheet poking her in the nose until he apologized and withdrew it.

'Something wrong with my review?' she asked.

'It's fine. Better than fine. We'll get to that later, too.'

'I see.' She was thoughtful. The silver fish suspicions had surfaced.

'Of course you do get things mixed up. I mean throwing in other things...'

'Other things?' Those yellow sheets. She was certain then. She felt a peculiar joy.

'This,' Jonathan said, pulling a sheaf of papers from his breast pocket, 'this is an article I've just written. I'm going to run it in the *Greenhill Sentinel*. Front page! Banner head! I may even get out an extra. Unless...' He grinned suddenly. 'But that's for later, too. First...'

'First?'

'Evidence.' He waved a single sheet at her. 'A copy of a letter to the Greenhill P.T.A from Chuck Lane.'

'I don't believe I'm interested in him right now,' she said.

She was shocked to discover that what had begun as an outright lie was suddenly an outright truth. She felt she had betrayed her deepest self. It still remained the outright truth. She was, at that moment, not at all interested in Chuck Lane. She had to fight an urgent need to smooth Jonathan's russet hair which was beginning to curl. She managed, but with effort, to keep her hands in her lap.

'You'll notice, if you look closely, that the L is crooked.' He shuffled some sheets, read, 'Dear Dorrie didn't like being the other woman.'

'There's no capital L in that,' Kay said coolly.

'Oh, I guess not. But it's in there some place. And anyhow, it proves my point. Those pages, and the letter to the P.T.A were typed on the same machine.'

'Interesting,' Kay said, savouring her peculiar joy.

'And now...my article.' His deep drawl was suddenly silky. He asked, with rhetorical flourish, 'The title? Who Is Chuck Lane?' He paused.

'Now wait,' she whispered.

He went on, 'Who Is Chuck Lane? He is a woman!'

'Jonathan, wait a minute,' she whispered.

Again he went on, 'A Greenhill woman.

One that many of us, most of us, know. She has been active in the P.T.A, in the Thespians, in everything. She has a small son. She is a divorcee. She writes, yes, but that's not all. She works harder than anyone imagines. She maintains her home, raises her son, and, probably locked in her lonely bedroom, filling the lonely nights, she writes.'

'Kitchen,' Kay said indignantly. 'And I'm not...'

He ignored the correction. 'Writes books about men and women. Books about life and love. She is a pretty good writer. She could be better. She would be a better writer if she weren't a phony, an icicle, and a prude.'

'A prude?' She was even more indignant.

'Prude.' He continued. 'She is, also, the woman I love. The end!' He stopped, hazel eyes defiant. 'What do you think about that?'

She considered. She brushed red-gold bangs from her brow. She set aside the book on her lap. She raised her dimpled chin, and her amber eyes. 'Well,' she said finally, 'you're a pretty good writer. You could be better if...'

He stared at her, dumbstruck. 'Aren't

you going to deny it? Aren't you going to argue with me? Aren't you going to swear that you're not Chuck Lane and never were and give a chance to...'

She cut in, 'Jonathan, should I?'

'I guess not. You don't have a leg to stand on. So that's what I put on the front page of the *Greenhill Sentinel.* Unless...'

'Unless?' It was wonderful that he knew. The particular elation that she had always missed was upon her. Still, Chuck Lane, and all his works, seemed dim and far away. 'Unless?' Kay repeated.

'Unless you marry me, of course.'

She said severely, 'That's blackmail, Jonathan.'

He bent over her. 'More blackmail. Kiss me, Kay Barrenger, or I'll tell the world.'

She touched her lips to his cheek. A sweet shock went through her.

'Not like that,' he said. 'You know better. I already know you know better. After all, I've read your books.'

'I am a scared, innocent little girl,' she told him. 'I think you'd better show me how.'

He showed her how.

There was, she thought delightedly, definitely something *there.*

329

While he kissed her, she stealthily drew his article from between his limp fingers. Body softening to his, she tore it to bits. It fell like snow from her prickling hands.

His arms closed around her. They filled the sofa together. Before she forgot to think, she decided that Chuck Lane's new book would not be called *Hungry* after all. It would be named *Satisfied*. And it would be the best one he ever wrote.